Great Women Comedians

Other Books in the History Makers Series:

America's Founders
Artists of the Renaissance
Astronauts
Cartoonists
Civil War Generals of the Confederacy
Civil War Generals of the Union
Cult Leaders
Dictators
Disease Detectives
Fighters Against American Slavery
Gangsters
Great Authors of Children's Literature
Great Composers
Great Conquerors
Great Male Comedians
Gunfighters
Home Run Kings
Influential First Ladies
The Kennedys
Leaders of Ancient Greece
Leaders of Black Civil Rights
Leaders of Women's Suffrage
Magicians and Illusionists
Male Olympic Champions
Native American Chiefs and Warriors
Pioneers of the American West
Pirates
Polar Explorers
Presidential Assassins
Presidents and Scandals
Rock and Roll Legends
Rulers of Ancient Egypt
Rulers of Ancient Rome
Scientists of Ancient Greece
Serial Killers
Spies
Twentieth-Century American Writers
Women Inventors
Women Leaders of Nations
Women of the American Revolution
Women Olympic Champions
Women Pop Stars

*History*MAKERS

Great Women Comedians

By Gail B. Stewart

LUCENT BOOKS
SAN DIEGO, CALIFORNIA

THOMSON
★
™
GALE

Detroit • New York • San Diego • San Francisco
Boston • New Haven, Conn. • Waterville, Maine
London • Munich

Library of Congress Cataloging-in-Publication Data
Stewart, Gail, 1949–
  Great women comedians / by Gail B. Stewart.
     p.   cm. — (History makers)
Includes bibliographical references and index.
Summary: Discusses the careers of such women as Gracie Allen, Lucille
Ball, Whoopi Goldberg, Roseanne, and Ellen DeGeneres and the impact
they had on comedy.
  ISBN 1-56006-953-8 (hardback; alk. paper)
  1. Women comedians—United States—Biography—Juvenile literature. [1.
Comedians. 2. Women—Biography.] I. Title. II. Series.
  PN2285 .S7265 2002
  792.7'028'0820973—dc21

2001005695

CONTENTS

FOREWORD

The literary form most often referred to as "multiple biography" was perfected in the first century A.D. by Plutarch, a perceptive and talented moralist and historian who hailed from the small town of Chaeronea in central Greece. His most famous work, *Parallel Lives*, consists of a long series of biographies of noteworthy ancient Greek and Roman statesmen and military leaders. Frequently, Plutarch compares a famous Greek to a famous Roman, pointing out similarities in personality and achievements. These expertly constructed and very readable tracts provided later historians and others, including playwrights like Shakespeare, with priceless information about prominent ancient personages and also inspired new generations of writers to tackle the multiple biography genre.

The Lucent History Makers series proudly carries on the venerable tradition handed down from Plutarch. Each volume in the series consists of a set of five to eight biographies of important and influential historical figures who were linked together by a common factor. In *Rulers of Ancient Rome*, for example, all the figures were generals, consuls, or emperors of either the Roman Republic or Empire; while the subjects of *Fighters Against American Slavery*, though they lived in different places and times, all shared the same goal, namely the eradication of human servitude. Mindful that politicians and military leaders are not (and never have been) the only people who shape the course of history, the editors of the series have also included representatives from a wide range of endeavors, including scientists, artists, writers, philosophers, religious leaders, and sports figures.

Each book is intended to give a range of figures—some well known, others less known; some who made a great impact on history, others who made only a small impact. For instance, by making Columbus's initial voyage possible, Spain's Queen Isabella I, featured in *Women Leaders of Nations*, helped to open up the New World to exploration and exploitation by the European powers. Inarguably, therefore, she made a major contribution to a series of events that had momentous consequences for the entire world. By contrast, Catherine II, the eighteenth-century Russian queen, and Golda Meir, the modern Israeli prime minister, did not play roles of global impact; however, their policies and actions significantly influenced the historical development of both their own countries and their regional neighbors. Regardless of their relative importance in the greater historical scheme, all of the figures chronicled in the History Makers series made contributions to posterity; and their public achievements, as well as what is known about their private lives, are presented and evaluated in light of the most recent scholarship.

In addition, each volume in the series is documented and substantiated by a wide array of primary and secondary source quotations. The primary source quotes enliven the text by presenting eyewitness views of the times and culture in which each history maker lived; while the secondary source quotes, taken from the works of respected modern scholars, offer expert elaboration and/ or critical commentary. Each quote is footnoted, demonstrating to the reader exactly where biographers find their information. The footnotes also provide the reader with the means of conducting additional research. Finally, to further guide and illuminate readers, each volume in the series features photographs, two bibliographies, and a comprehensive index.

The History Makers series provides both students engaged in research and more casual readers with informative, enlightening, and entertaining overviews of individuals from a variety of circumstances, professions, and backgrounds. No doubt all of them, whether loved or hated, benevolent or cruel, constructive or destructive, will remain endlessly fascinating to each new generation seeking to identify the forces that shaped their world.

The Rule Breakers

Being a comedian is a difficult job—far more so than one might imagine. In fact, there is an old saying about the business—so old that no one knows who said it first: Dying is easy, comedy is hard. Comedy is risk—it is standing in front of a room of strangers and sharing thoughts. It is hoping that a story, a quip, or even a funny face will make people laugh. The laughter of strangers determines whether a comedian is good or not. Comedy is one of the only performance arts in which excellence is based solely on an audience's reaction.

"About as Comical as a Crutch"

Comedy is also the only performance art that continues to be dominated by men, although women's numbers have risen somewhat in the past few years. "Where they were once below 1 percent of stand-up comics," wrote historian Susan Horowitz in 1997, "women are now 15–20 percent of the profession." [1]

Why are women so underrepresented? Experts point to a number of reasons. One is that for centuries, many people believed that women did not have either the skill or the temperament to tell a joke or think of a witty remark. In *Graham* magazine, which was quite popular in Europe and the United States during the nineteenth century, one writer tried to explain:

> Women have a sprightliness, cleverness, smartness, though but little wit. There is a body and substance in true wit, with a reflectiveness rarely found apart from a masculine intellect. . . . We know of no one writer of the other sex, that has a high character for humor. . . . The female character doesn't admit of it. [2]

So common was this view that many women themselves believed it to be true. One woman wrote in 1922, "To men belong of right the more obvious sorts [of humor]; the witty speech, full of ridicule, irony, and satire; the rollicking joke; the jest . . . and last, the funny story!" [3] A male writer, annoyed in 1909 by someone's suggestion that a woman might be capable of humor, insisted, "Measured by the ordinary standards of humor, she is about as comical as a crutch. . . . A woman was made to be loved and fondled . . . she certainly was not made to be laughed at."[4]

Unladylike

Even if a woman had wanted to be comical in the first years of the twentieth century, she would have had to fight cultural taboos against it. It was unladylike for a woman to want to make others laugh, warned social commentator Elizabeth Trotter in a *New Republic* article of 1922, and for a woman to be known as a humorist would be the height of embarrassment. "It is a fact," said Trotter, "that no woman covets [the label of 'humorist'] at its present value, or could have it bestowed upon her without being shamefaced about it."[5]

The shame of being a comedian, or even being considered funny, applied even to literature. Although several women in the early twentieth century wrote humorous essays or stories, they did so under fictitious names. One of these was the American poet Edna St. Vincent Millay, who worried that she would not be taken seriously as a poet if people knew she wrote humor. Therefore, when she completed her collection of satirical, humorous sketches about marriage and society in 1924, she published it under the name Nancy Boyd.

Edna St. Vincent Millay wrote humorous stories under a fictitious name to protect her reputation as a serious poet.

If even *writing* humorous material could threaten a woman's reputation, performing comedy on stage was a far greater risk. Women who did were often dismissed as mannish or odd. "Since the accepted idea of a sexy woman was the shy, ingenue type," explains one historian, "it followed that most women connected being kooky with being unattractive, and the only thing that would compel a female to [do comedy] was a 'sense of desperation.'"[6]

Even as late as the 1980s, women believed that men considered humor unfeminine. Gilda Radner, who achieved a great deal of success on NBC's *Saturday Night Live,* remarked, "I know I've scared many men off because of humor. I'll be funny instead of feminine. You're not likely to see me sitting at the back of a party being pretty." [7]

There were a few exceptions, of course. Audiences tended to accept women used in comedy sketches, especially if they "played dumb" or were attractive—and even better, sexy. Early comedy acts that featured a pretty woman acting as the butt of her male partner's ribbing were well received. But a woman doing a solo act, wisecracking her way through a monologue, was something audiences were not yet ready for.

Gilda Radner was a successful comedian during the 1980s despite the restraints that society placed on women comics at the time.

Raising the Bar

Fortunately, the world at the beginning of the twenty-first century is quite different. Women comedians in ever-increasing numbers are appearing in comedy clubs, movies, and even their own television shows. No subject matter seems taboo; some women joke about their husbands or children, others speak openly about being lesbians, African Americans, Koreans, or soccer moms.

What accounts for such a change in the past hundred years? Certainly a big reason is social change outside of show business—the destruction of stereotypes of women and the strides women have made toward equality in other areas of employment. "Society has had to wake up to the fact that women could be surgeons, police officers, mechanics, and just about everything else," says one comedy club fan. "Add 'comedian' to the list, too." [8]

But over the years a great deal of change was also brought about *within* the comedy field—by a number of women who became comedians despite the obstacles. Gracie Allen, Lucille Ball, Whoopi Goldberg, Roseanne, and Ellen DeGeneres are five of these women. Each of them became a highly successful comedian, despite the restraints society attached to women comics during various eras. Some restraints had to do with appearance, others with style or the subject matter of the act.

Each of these pioneers was able to change something, to break new ground in comedy. Some changes were dramatic, others very subtle. But no matter how these women accomplished these changes, each one opened up new possibilities for the generations of comedians that have come after her.

CHAPTER 1

Gracie Allen

Gracie Allen was a comedian who got her start in the days of vaudeville. At the beginning of the twentieth century, before movies became popular, and before the advent of television, theater owners booked groups of acts to come to their city. An act might be a magician, a singer, or a dancer. It might be a comic—people loved watching comedy acts.

Gracie Allen, who with her husband, George Burns, formed the comedy team of Burns and Allen, not only was a success in vaudeville, but also achieved stardom in films, on radio, and on television. Few entertainers of any sort could boast being headliners in four different media over a period of thirty-five years. And the type of comedy for which Allen was so well known was a style all her own—and has been copied by a host of comedians who came after her.

Roots in Vaudeville

Grace Ethel Cecile Rosalie Allen was born in San Francisco, California, on July 26, 1906, just a few months after the famous earthquake. Her father, George Allen, was a song and dance man who had performed in minstrel shows as a teenager. (Minstrel shows were a type of entertainment popular in the mid- to late 1800s in which white singers and dancers would blacken their faces with makeup and perform as blacks.) George Allen also ran a dance school out of their home. His specialty was Irish dancing, and he often traveled up and down the West Coast performing his songs and dances.

Gracie's mother had never been in show business, but loved music and dancing. Before Gracie was born, the Allens lived next door to a well-known opera singer named Alice Nielson. While pregnant with Gracie, her mother would go next door and listen to Nielson practice, hoping that her unborn child would also develop a beautiful voice.

Gracie had three sisters, Hazel, Pearl, and Bessie, and their parents were able to instill a love of performing in all of their daughters. Their father taught them to dance and to enjoy being in front of an audience. Their mother sewed beautiful costumes they wore for dancing school—although George downplayed the value of fancy costumes. "You'll never make a nickel all dolled up in a spangled skirt," he told them. "If you're going to get anywhere in show business, you have to be a character."[9] It was advice that Gracie would remember.

"My Heart Was Somewhere Else"

The Allen home was an elegant three-story house in San Francisco. It was unusual in several ways; for one, it had the first marble bathroom in the city. Its backyard held a canary-filled aviary and a small gymnasium. Not surprisingly, the Allen house was a social hall for the neighborhood and the scene for many parties.

George taught his dancing classes in the basement, which ran the length of the house and had a redwood floor. When they got older, Bessie and Pearl gave music and dancing lessons in the house, too. There was no doubt that the family had musical talent. Gracie later remarked that she always felt inferior when it came to dancing, however. "I was the only one who was no great dancer," she said. "My heart was somewhere else."[10]

Gracie Allen, seen here in a 1912 photo, first performed onstage at age three.

She was only three when her father took her onstage for the very first time and she first discovered what she really loved. She was to perform an interpretive Irish dance at a church social. Wearing a man's coat and top hat, and with a long, red beard fastened under her chin, Gracie was supposed to be an elf. However, she hated the beard because it was scratchy. In the middle of the dance, she took it off and draped it over her arm.

The crowd loved it, and Gracie heard the roar of laughter and applause for the first time in her life. The following day, she was proud to learn that she was the only one in the event who received a mention in the local newspaper. She later wrote, "I was a character—and just as Daddy said, a character is always a hit."[11]

Setbacks

Gracie endured two very difficult times when she was young. The first happened when she was about four. She had been left in the care of her sister Bessie. When the doorbell rang and Bessie ran to answer it, Gracie accidentally pulled a pot of boiling water onto her shoulder and arm.

She was severely burned, and initially, doctors thought they might have to amputate the arm, for it became infected. She eventually healed; however, the muscles had been damaged and were quite weak. She used a punching bag as she got older, trying to regain as much strength as she could in her arm. But throughout the rest of her life, she was very self-conscious about the scarring, and she never wore anything without long sleeves.

Despite being abandoned by her father as a young girl, Gracie developed into a strong and confident young woman.

The second setback was being abandoned by her father. He left town just before she began school and never returned to the family. Gracie had idolized him and felt betrayed by his leaving without a word or letter of good-bye to his wife or daughters.

Either of these events—her father's abandonment or her severe burns—could have turned the little girl into a painfully shy, unsmiling young woman. But Gracie was strong and confident, and although these incidents were painful, they would not keep her from seeking what she wanted most: a career on stage.

Interests Other than School

Gracie attended a Catholic convent school in San Francisco called Star of the Sea. Her mother, who eventually married a city police captain, hoped her daughter would do well in school. However, it seemed right away that academics would not be her strength.

The little girl was far more interested in walking downtown after school was dismissed and looking at the posters of entertainers displayed in front of the theaters. She daydreamed about her own photograph being displayed in front of a theater someday and excitedly told her sisters about her ambition.

Pearl was especially exasperated by the daily detours past the theaters and told her little sister her daydreaming was a waste of time. Her mother, however, was more understanding. Perhaps she could see how eager Gracie was to perform—just as her father once had. She allowed Gracie to save her money and attend matinees whenever she could.

One of the high points during that time was meeting one of the world's greatest comics. Charlie Chaplin was making a movie in the San Francisco area, and Gracie's stepfather happened to meet him. On her birthday, her stepfather gave her a choice of presents: would she like to go on an airplane ride to Chicago or meet Charlie Chaplin? She excitedly chose meeting Chaplin.

The Four Colleens

In the days of vaudeville, aspiring entertainers could go to a music publisher's office and learn a song free of charge. (The publishers hoped that new songs would get used in acts and become more popular.) Allen could not make the rounds of publishers' offices while school was in session, so she was delighted when summer vacation came along.

She later recalled that process:

> I couldn't wait to get out of school. I lived for vacations. I may not have known the name of any streets in San Francisco, but I knew where every song publisher was. I'd go to their offices long before vacation came, learn some new song, design myself some new costume, and the minute school was out, run to a lady in one of the booking offices who'd find engagements for me.[12]

A frequent job she had as a young teenager was singing for a few minutes to entertain audiences during intermission at early movies. She had help from both Hazel and her mother, who assisted her with her costumes.

When Allen was fourteen, she and her sisters worked up a harmony singing and dancing act, calling themselves The Four Colleens. In their act, the girls would appear out of a mist and do a highland reel—and after it was done, they'd disappear into the mist. During one performance, Allen slipped on some talcum powder left on the stage and when she fell, she accidentally pulled her sisters down with her. Thinking it was a part of the act, the audience howled. Ironically, they performed the next four shows perfectly and were subsequently fired for leaving out the laughs.

"Larry, Look Out!"

Gracie left school after turning sixteen, and she auditioned for a part in the Larry Reilly Company—a vaudeville act much like her father's old one, with Irish dances and songs. She got the job, but because she was still a teenager, Reilly invited Bessie and Hazel to join the act. They had talent, which would benefit his act, and in addition, they could keep an eye on their younger sister.

Reilly and the Allen sisters set off for Chicago for the first stop of their tour. Chicago audiences loved the act. Allen later remembered how proud she was when a local critic praised their act, writing, "Larry, look out! The girls are stealing the show!" [13]

The tour eventually landed in New York City, and by this time, Hazel and Bessie felt that Gracie would do fine on her own. Hazel would return to San Francisco to help Pearl with the dancing school, and Bessie was going to get married. But no sooner had they left than Larry Reilly got a better job and left, too. Gracie was alone in New York with very little money and no prospects.

A Fortunate Meeting

Allen made the rounds of theaters in New York, but found nothing that appealed to her. An actor named Benny Ryan, whom Allen dated, wrote an act that she could use, but it required about three hundred dollars' worth of props and scenery, as well as a male partner. She had neither and opted instead to start secretarial school so she could earn a steady income.

Living in a rooming house with two other girls who were in show business, she heard them one day discussing two comedians who needed partners. George Burns and Billy Lorraine had a vaudeville act in which they impersonated popular Broadway stars such as Al Jolson, George M. Cohan, and Eddie Cantor. But Burns and Lorraine were soon going to break up their act, and each was looking for a new partner.

Allen decided to come to their show to decide whether she was interested in working with either man. After being introduced to George Burns offstage, she was instantly struck by how charming he was. He found her extremely engaging, too. The two quickly decided to work up an act and take it on the road.

16

A Switch

At first, Allen thought that the two of them could use the act that Benny Ryan had written for her. However, neither she nor Burns had the three hundred dollars needed for the props. Besides, Burns had already written an act for himself and a partner, so they decided to start out with his script. In this act, George had given himself all the funny dialogue, with Gracie playing what was called the "straight man"—the one who set up the situation for the funny man.

They opened in Boonton, New Jersey—a one-night stand that would pay a total of ten dollars. Things did not go well at first. Both of them realized that his funny lines were not getting the laughs that her straight lines were. At first, they assumed that the audience just didn't get the gags. But Burns realized that it wasn't that at all; it was simply that the audience was drawn to Allen's personality. They loved her.

Allen met George Burns when the young comedian was looking for a new stage partner.

Immediately after the first show, Burns rewrote the script backstage, giving Allen the funny lines and making himself the straight man. This was a first in a man-woman act, because it was always the man who was the comedian.

"Illogical Logic"

Allen fell into the role of playing a ditzy, charming woman who never seemed to get anything straight. It was a takeoff on the Dumb Dora type of character—the woman who was so foolish she couldn't understand anything. Gracie's character, however, would be engaging and immensely likable.

17

This would be her trademark—her own style of comedy that audiences would find both funny and touching. As Burns explained Allen's role, "The character was simply the dizziest dame in the world, but she differed from other 'Dumb Doras' because Gracie played her as if she were totally sane, as if her answers actually made sense."[14]

The character that Burns created for her used what they called "illogical logic." For instance, Allen might explain how she put salt in the pepper shaker and pepper in the salt shaker—her logic being that if they ever got mixed up, they would come out right. The idea was wrong, explained Burns, but it was close to right. Another of her thoughts was that if she shortened the ironing and vacuum cleaner cords, she could save electricity. Every gag made sense in a convoluted way.

Burns claimed years later that theirs was one of the only man-woman comedy acts that didn't need to resort to sarcasm and didn't need funny clothes to be funny. The character of Gracie was sweet and earnest; George's character was simply the exasperated, cigar-chomping man in a plain suit. And audiences couldn't get enough of them.

They had started as what was known then as a "disappointment act," a last-minute fill-in for any act that failed to show up. "Every Monday and Thursday we packed our bags and sat beside our telephones," recalled Allen, "so that if some other act missed connections or broke a leg we'd be ready to substitute. There were lots of theaters running vaudeville in those days, lots of actors and lots of broken legs."[15] By 1926, they were getting regular bookings and attracted large numbers of fans.

"Dizzy"

Most of their routines began with the two of them walking on stage, holding hands. They'd talk for a few minutes and then sing and do a soft-shoe dance. One of their favorite routines was called "Dizzy," and like all of their comedy it involved George being perplexed by the way Gracie's mind worked. In one part of "Dizzy," Gracie suggests that they do a crossword puzzle:

George: That would be fun.

Gracie: I'm very good at them now. You know, I make them up.

George: Well, make one up.

Gracie: All right. What is it that starts with *c* and, uh,

well, I don't know how many letters, what is it?

George: Hmm, that's very good. You made that up.

Gracie: That came right out of my own head.

George: I'd have it stuffed.

Gracie: My head?

George: Your head.

Gracie: Oh, I have brains, you know.

George: Have you?

Gracie: Oh, I have brains I haven't even used yet.

Audiences were drawn to Allen's ditzy but charming onstage persona and playful interaction with straight-man George Burns.

George: I see. Well, leave 'em alone. Don't disturb them. . . . It starts with *c* and you don't know how many letters, what is it. Does it jump?

Gracie: No.

George: Does it swim?

Gracie: No.

George: That's all right. Now give me another one.

Gracie: Well, no, you didn't guess that one.

George: I give up.

Gracie: Well, look. Men shave with it.

George: And it starts with *c*.

Gracie: Yes.

George: Well, the only thing that I can think of that a man shaves with is soap.

Gracie: Soap! That's it. That's very good, George. Now you make one up.

George: Why don't you go to a doctor and have him examine your head, and if the doctor finds a brain, have somebody examine the doctor. [16]

More than a Comedy Twosome

Although they had liked each other right from the beginning, Burns and Allen were not romantically involved. Grace still dated Benny Ryan and even thought about marrying him someday. George, though not serious about any one person, dated several young women. However, something happened on the way to San Francisco that was to change things between them.

Gracie was looking forward to playing in San Francisco; performing in front of so many family members and friends was an exciting prospect. However, she was becoming concerned about what she had first thought was stage fright jitters. A nervous stomach had developed into an intense pain. She could no longer ignore it and soon was taken to the hospital with appendicitis.

Instead of delivering her long-awaited hometown performance, Allen was in the hospital. Burns was at her side constantly, bringing her flowers and keeping her company. By the time she had recuperated and was back on tour with him, it was apparent to their close friends that he had fallen in love with her. Allen, who still had feelings

Burns and Allen's popular weekly radio show aired for nearly twenty years.

for Benny Ryan, was unsure of her feelings for George, and that made him more miserable as each day passed on their tour.

Finally, Allen later recalled, he gave her an ultimatum—either marry him or the act would split up. She thought about it for several hours and decided she did love him. They married quickly, finding a justice of the peace who was on his way out the door to go fishing. "He had his reel and basket, and paraphernalia," Allen laughed, "and was about to make a quick exit when we arrived. He had to stop and marry us, which I'm sure didn't take long, because when we got downstairs the taxi meter had only registered fifteen cents!" [17]

Moving into Radio

The success of the couple's act coincided with vaudeville's decline. By the end of the 1920s, vaudeville was almost dead, and Burns and Allen were one of the top comedy acts in the nation. They were asked to appear in London for twenty-six weeks and were well received there.

In 1931, Burns and Allen were invited to appear with Eddie Cantor on his popular radio show. The audience loved them, and soon they were being asked to appear on other radio shows. Within one year, they were given their own radio show. The increased income allowed them to buy their first home after living for so many years in hotels. With the stability of a home, they started a family, too. They adopted a daughter named Sandra Jean in 1934; a year later they adopted a son, Ronald John.

Allen performs a radio publicity stunt called "Piano Concerto for Index Finger."

New Challenges

However, even though they had a steady income and were no longer constantly on the road, they both found that having a weekly radio show was difficult work. One thing that was different was the need for new, fresh material on a weekly basis. When they were in vaudeville, they could use the same routines for months, since they rarely played to the same audiences.

Now that they were on national radio, however, they could hardly repeat the same bits week after week. To keep up, they hired five writers to turn out gags in the standard formula that had been working so well. For example, in one routine, Gracie is consoling George, who is complaining about his problems:

> Gracie: All great singers have their trials; look at Caruso. Thirty years on a desert island with all those cannibals.
>
> George: You've got the wrong man.
>
> Gracie: No, you're the man for me.
>
> George: But they say I'm through as a singer. I'm extinct.
>
> Gracie: You do not. [18]

One-Finger Concertos and a Run for President

Even though their radio show did well in the ratings, Burns and Allen occasionally engaged in a publicity stunt, just to keep the audiences guessing. In every one of them, Gracie was the main focus. In 1940, a presidential election year, George came up with the idea of Allen running for president on the Surprise Party ticket. Her slogan was, "Down with common sense! Vote for Gracie."

She even had a train with a campaign platform, and the front of the train was emblazened with the party mascot—a kangaroo, because of the campaign's motto: "It's in the bag." She was interviewed by reporters from around the country. Staying in character as Gracie, she answered questions about the national debt: "It's something to be proud of—it's the biggest in the world, isn't it?" And about foreign relations, she responded, "They're all right with me, but when they come, they've just got to bring their own bedding." [19] Allen was surprised when told that in November, she'd actually received several hundred write-in votes.

Another publicity stunt was a musical work she had supposedly composed, called "The Piano Concerto for Index Finger." She and Burns referred to the piece so many times that audiences wondered when they would ever hear it on their program. Finally, their musical director wrote a concerto for Allen; she had only one note during the entire piece. She was even asked to play it at Carnegie Hall and eventually made appearances with famed conductor Arthur Fiedler and the Boston Pops.

"Before Every Performance . . . Panicky!"

While the publicity stunts and guest appearances were fun for audiences, secretly Allen was unhappy. She had always suffered from stage fright, and even standing in front of a microphone doing the radio show terrified her. She and Burns had done a few films, and she'd even been talked into doing a few without him. But it was not enjoyable for her. Although Allen gave the appearance of being totally comfortable, she later acknowledged that she was anything but:

> The on-stage Gracie may look poised and steady, but the real Gracie is shy, a little self-conscious, and before every performance of my life, panicky! I've played five and six performances a day on tour and before each curtain rose I've had that strange tenseness we call stage fright and when I'm through, my hands are wet. Other performers do their radio shows with the house lights on, but not me. If I saw an audience, I'd be through.[20]

For this reason, Allen fought against the idea of moving to the newest medium—television. But Burns was excited by the prospect in 1950, and Allen eventually agreed, although she found it physically draining. She worried that she would forget her lines and found that the cameras made her more nervous. Even so, she did very well, and audiences found Burns and Allen as enjoyable on television as they had on radio.

"Say Goodnight, Gracie"

The television show was very popular, attracting as many as 30 million viewers each week. Once again, just as their radio show had imitated their vaudeville show, the television show was based on the same two characters—a lovable but slightly off-base Gracie with her long-suffering husband, George.

Although the show shared some similarities with comedies such as *I Love Lucy*—involving a wife getting into predicaments trying to fool her husband, for instance—it was also unique in that George, who was very much a member of the cast, was also the narrator. He would appear on-screen at the beginning of the show and speculate about what Gracie was up to at that moment, and then he would

Allen and Burns prepare for a scene on the set of their long-running TV series, The George Burns and Gracie Allen Show.

walk into his den on-screen and watch television. The audience would then follow the action with him.

The most popular part of the show came at the end, when Burns and Allen would come out onto the stage for a moment of their old vaudeville-style banter. They might discuss one of her relatives—long a subject of their act—or a misconception Gracie had. For instance, one of the show's sponsors was Carnation Milk, and she wondered aloud how they got milk from carnations. After a few minutes of this, Burns would always smile and say, "Say goodnight, Gracie." [21] She'd turn to the audience and say, "Goodnight." Every show ended the same way, and the phrase "Say goodnight, Gracie" became firmly entrenched in the pop culture of the 1950s.

In 1958, after eight years, the show went off the air. Allen had been struggling with heart trouble and migraine headaches for some time, and her doctors worried that the stress of working was not good for her. She died in her sleep of a heart attack on August 27, 1964.

Gracie Allen's career made history. The role she took for herself was definitely "dizzy," as her husband, George Burns called her part of the act. However, it was a much fuller, more human version of the dumb blond stereotype. Her humor, said critics, was based on the little details of language that led to misunderstandings.

Even more remarkable was the way she adapted her career so successfully from vaudeville to radio, and from radio to television. It is understandable why the American Women in Radio and Television Association names their yearly prize for excellence in the electronic media the Gracie Allen Award.

CHAPTER 2

Lucille Ball

No woman comic has been as beloved to audiences and as respected by other comedians as Lucille Ball. It is said that her face is more recognizable than any other on the planet. Her television shows are entertaining a third generation of fans in eighty countries around the world.

Lucille Ball shattered stereotypes about women in comedy. She was a very attractive woman who could do slapstick and contort her face as though it were made of rubber—without sacrificing her femininity. *I Love Lucy*, the television series she did with her husband, Desi Arnaz, was a sensation and became a yardstick against which all other television comedies would be measured.

"I Do Remember Everything That Happened"

Lucille Desiree Ball was born on August 6, 1911, in Jamestown, New York. Her father, Henry, who was just seventeen when his daughter was born, was a telephone lineman. Her mother, Desiree, was an accomplished piano player who had once dreamed of pursuing a career as a concert pianist.

When Lucille was just a baby, Henry decided to move the family west, to Butte, Montana. There were jobs in the copper mines there. But mining was an extremely difficult occupation; mines were cold, drafty, and damp. Within three years, Henry had contracted a severe case of pneumonia. He was too ill and weak to continue working, so the young family packed up their belongings and headed back to New York.

But Henry was far sicker than he realized. They had gone as far as Michigan when his fever

Lucille Desiree Ball in 1912, at age eight months.

and labored breathing made traveling impossible. The family stayed with friends in Michigan to let Henry recuperate, but in his rundown state he caught an even more virulent disease: typhoid fever. At the age of twenty-three, Henry died, leaving a four-year-old daughter and a wife who was four months pregnant.

Many years later, Ball said that her father's death was the earliest memory she had. "I do remember everything that happened," she said. "Hanging out the window, begging to play with the kids next door who had measles . . . the doctor coming, my mother weeping. I remember a bird that flew in the window, a picture that fell off the wall." [22]

The bird flying into the house must have been an especially vivid memory, for throughout her life, Ball could not bear the sight of pictures of birds. She could not stay in a hotel room, for example, that had pictures of birds on the walls; she would remove them or have an assistant do it.

Lucille enjoyed slapstick comedy even as a young girl.

"I Wanted to Make People Laugh"

Little Lucille and her mother headed to New York soon afterward. Desiree's parents, Fred and Florabelle Hunt, lived in the town of Celoron, near Jamestown; they were happy to have their daughter and grandchild—soon to be grandchildren, when Lucille's brother Freddie was born—so near.

It was while living with her grandparents that Lucille began to feel the lure of show business. Grandpa Hunt would regularly take Lucille and Freddie into Jamestown to see vaudeville shows on Saturday nights. Lucille enjoyed it all, but the comedy—largely slapstick—was her favorite. "[Grandpa] was a devotee," she later said, "and we loved it, too. All I know is that I wanted to make people laugh." [23]

Upheaval

But the security and happiness Lucille and her family had found after Henry's death changed abruptly in 1917. The United States entered World War I, and workers were desperately needed in factories to make weapons, ammunition, uniforms, and boots for soldiers. Women who had never worked outside the home before were urged to apply for full-time employment helping the American war effort.

Desiree was no exception, and at her new job she met Ed Peterson, who became her second husband. Peterson was indifferent to his two young stepchildren; he told Desiree he did not want them to call him Daddy, for they were not his children. Lucille and Freddie could sense that he did not care for them, and avoided him as often as possible.

While in high school, Lucille directed and starred in a comedy called Charley's Aunt.

Soon after the marriage, Peterson took a job in Detroit and urged his new wife to accompany him. The job was supposed to last six months, and since Lucille was already in school, it was decided that she stay behind and live with Peterson's parents. Sophia Peterson was nothing like Lucille's other grandmother; she was a stern, forbidding woman with little sense of humor. She wanted Lucille to become a God-fearing woman and insisted that she wear dowdy, long dresses and tie her hair back in a tight bun. She even insisted that Lucille not have mirrors, for she believed they would make the little girl vain. Years later, Ball would recall that she was unhappy not being able to relate to the Petersons. "It gave me a feeling of frustration," she said, "and of reaching out and trying to please." [24]

"The Wonderful Feeling"

Desiree was also miserable; she had discovered that Ed was both a gambler and an alcoholic. She soon left Detroit, divorced him, and, with her children, moved back into her parents' house. Lucille was elated, and life improved almost immediately.

She became more involved with school plays; in high school, she had the lead in a comedy called *Charley's Aunt* and, she later recalled, she could take credit for almost the entire production:

> [I] felt for the first time the wonderful feeling that comes from getting real laughs on a stage. I not only played the male lead, [I] directed it, cast it, sold tickets, printed the posters, swept up the stage afterwards, and turned out the lights. It was a great success. At twenty-five cents a ticket, we made $25 and gave all of it to the ninth grade class for a party. [25]

The success of that show encouraged her to learn as much as she could about performing. She hoped that eventually she could enter vaudeville and knew that having many different abilities would give her a better chance. She worked at piano lessons for a time, and although she did not have a real talent for it, she picked up enough from her lessons to play a little. She also learned a bit on the saxophone and the ukulele.

"Lucy's Wasting Her Time"

When she was fifteen, Lucille begged her mother to send her to New York, to the John Murray Anderson–Robert Milton Academy. Its focus was on theater and dance, and its reputation was excellent. It was, however, a very strict school. Students could not speak without permission, and the classes were extremely challenging.

Though she had insisted on attending this school, Lucille quickly became very shy and reserved. Performing for friends and classmates back in Celoron was quite different from being in front of some of the best drama instructors in the country. She couldn't speak up in class; even when called on, she could do nothing but stammer.

After a year, John Murray Anderson himself wrote a letter to her mother, explaining that Lucille was not cut out for performing. "Lucy's wasting her time and mine," he said. "She's too shy and reticent to put her best foot forward." [26] Unwilling to return home, however, Lucille remained in New York. She took odd jobs to support herself—as a salesclerk, selling hot dogs at an amusement park, and as a soda jerk at Walgreen's.

"As Untalented as They Come"

Not long afterward, she decided to try to find show business jobs on her own. She was a fair dancer and thought she could probably find work as a chorus girl. But after getting a few small parts and being dismissed soon afterward, she realized that directors expected a level of skill that she did not yet have. "I couldn't sing, dance, or perform in any way," Ball wrote later. "I was as untalented as they come. I couldn't even walk correctly. . . . I'd walk stiffly across the stage, and they'd say, 'Couldn't you walk more like a showgirl? You are a showgirl, you know.'" [27]

Ball took modeling classes when she could afford them, and her luck finally changed when she was offered a job as a Chesterfield cigarette girl. Her pictures appeared on billboards around town, and that exposure led to a modeling job with a noted dress designer in New York. She used the glamorous name Diane Belmont and dyed her dark hair blond.

During this time, Ball had a physical breakdown, collapsing on the runway during an important fashion show. Various explanations have been given—everything from malnutrition (she often starved herself to keep slim) to rheumatoid arthritis. Whatever the cause, she was confined to a wheelchair and went home to Celoron, where her mother nursed her back to health for the next two years.

Ball returned to New York in 1933, intending to get back into modeling. However, she soon met an agent looking for chorus girls for a new film being shot in Hollywood, called *Roman Scandals*. She caught the eye of the casting director and landed the part.

In the Movies

During the filming, Ball worked hard to overcome her former shyness. She knew this was finally her chance, and she didn't want to waste it. Perhaps the most important moment in her career came when the director asked which of the chorus girls was willing to take a mud pie in the face. She eagerly volunteered and insisted years later that her willingness to do anything, no matter how silly, got her noticed:

> I may not have been as beautiful as some of the other showgirls, but [the director] certainly noticed me. . . . There were spots where they needed a girl to scream or get chased by alligators. Some of the other girls were asked, and they said, "Why? That's a nothing bit!" But I was tickled to death. It gave me a chance to work [with the star] and to work longer on a scene. The director would say, "You need somebody to do what? Why don't we get that girl who ran through with the duck?" They knew I'd run, I'd scream, I'd fall—I'd do what I was asked to do. [28]

Her strategy worked, for she got a flurry of parts in other comedies, and worked with some of the most famous stars in Hollywood:

Ball worked alongside the famous Marx Brothers in the film Room Service.

the Marx Brothers, Laurel and Hardy, and the Three Stooges. The parts were not large by any standard, but she did well. Soon she had worked her way up to supporting roles in what were called "B" pictures—the second-rate, lower-budget Hollywood movies.

"Wham Bang"

By 1938, Ball had made seven films and was receiving positive comments from critics. She had even dyed her hair bright red, hoping to get noticed by directors, and it seemed to be working. Even so, she was discouraged that she could not work her way into the higher-budget movies. What would it take, she wondered, to star in an "A" movie? She seemed to be getting no closer to that goal as she continued to do "B" movies—occasionally even getting top billing.

In 1940, for instance, she got the lead in *Too Many Girls*, playing a spoiled heiress named Connie Casey. In the film, Connie's father hires four football players to protect his daughter while she is away at school. One of the football players was portrayed by Desiderio Alberto Arnaz III, who in real life was a dashing Cuban bandleader also trying to get into the movie business.

Ball was attracted to him instantly. She said later, "I was wearing a slinky gold lamé dress slit up to my thigh, and I had a fake black eye. Because of my appearance, I'm sure he was not impressed. I was impressed with him, though, and I must admit that I fell in love with Desi, wham bang, in about five minutes." [29]

The two began dating during the filming of *Too Many Girls* and eloped soon afterward. They both had tempers, however, and since Arnaz had the reputation of being a playboy, some Hollywood gossips predicted the marriage would not last more than six weeks.

An Exciting New Medium

In many ways, those gossips were right; the marriage was in trouble almost from the beginning. Hints of Arnaz's unfaithfulness, plus Ball's fiery temper, resulted in constant fighting. By the time the film was finished and Arnaz and his band went back on the road, the two were barely speaking.

Ball compensated by throwing herself into work, making more films and for the first time, trying her hand at radio. In 1947, she landed a job on a popular CBS radio program called *My Favorite Husband,* playing a role that would prove to be quite similar to her character on *I Love Lucy.* But as satisfying as that success was, she

Ball (fourth from right) met and fell in love with Desi Arnaz (third from right) during the filming of Too Many Girls. *They eloped soon after.*

still felt that she had not really attained star status—her lifetime goal. And with Desi still touring with his band much of the year, her personal life was not a success either.

A solution to both problems surfaced in 1950. The medium of television was brand new, and networks were scrambling to produce new shows. For Ball, it seemed to offer a whole new start on her career. "I never cared much for myself in movies," she later said, "but I remember when I was first shown television, I thought, 'Now this is something I could get into.'" [30] She wanted to do a series of her own— a comedy similar to *My Favorite Husband*—and she wanted Arnaz as her costar. Working together on a project might even save their failing marriage.

A Hard Sell

The two approached CBS with the idea for their show, but the network was unwilling at first to cast Desi as the husband. Even though the two were married in real life, said executives, a Cuban with such a pronounced accent and a redheaded American woman would not seem a likely couple to audiences.

But Ball was unwilling to do the project without her husband, so the couple put together a musical comedy act and took it on the road, much like a vaudeville show. They called it "Desi Arnaz and Band with Lucille Ball." In their act Ball played the cello, imitated a seal, and sang a few duets with her husband. Audiences loved the act, but even after this, CBS was doubtful about casting Arnaz.

Unwilling to compromise, Ball and Arnaz scraped together sixteen thousand dollars and formed their own production company, which they named Desilu. They would produce the show, which would be called *I Love Lucy*, and Desilu would both take on the risk and retain ownership of each episode.

Pioneers

Several things about *I Love Lucy* made it a pioneer in the television industry. For example, the network assumed that Ball and Arnaz would be moving from their Hollywood home to New York to begin their show. In those days, shows were broadcast live from New York, where most television viewers were. People in the rest of the country would see shows aired later in kinescope, a process of filming directly off a television screen. So poor was the quality of kinescope, Ball explained, that images aired that way "looked like they were shot through linoleum." [31]

Neither Ball nor Arnaz was anxious to move from Hollywood, since she was now pregnant and wished to remain near home. At the

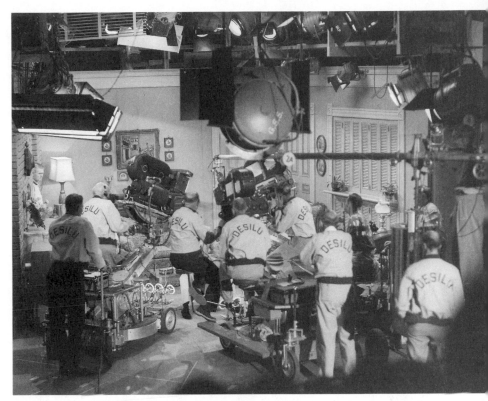

The filming of I Love Lucy *used three cameras that ran simultaneously, a technique that became known as "the Desilu method."*

same time, they did not want to sacrifice the quality of their show. They came up with a solution: to do the show on more expensive film recording. That way, it would be clear wherever it was shown, and since it would be prerecorded, it could be broadcast over and over— the birth of the rerun.

They wanted to use a live audience; Ball had enjoyed having an audience when she did her radio show because she felt she performed better. She insisted, however, that the lighting be different from what was normally used in television. She was forty years old, and harsh overhead lighting was not flattering, so the director came up with the idea of placing lights at the foot of the camera. This technique removed every shadow from her face.

Another first was the use of three cameras for filming *I Love Lucy*. One was for close-ups, another for medium shots, and the third for long shots. All three cameras were going simultaneously; afterward an editor would splice the best shots together. This system worked extraordinarily well; it became known as "the Desilu method" and was used by dozens of television shows that came later.

A National Pastime

On September 8, 1951—less than two months after their daughter, Lucie Desiree, was born—the first episode of *I Love Lucy* was shot. It was broadcast a month later, and audiences loved it. The show's premise was simple: Lucy (Ball) and Ricky (Arnaz) Ricardo lived in an apartment in New York City. He was a bandleader at the Tropicana Club, and she was a homemaker. Their landlords were Fred and Ethel Mertz, played by former vaudeville entertainer William Frawley and actor Vivian Vance; they would become best friends with the Ricardos.

When Ball became pregnant with her second child, the creative team wrote a pregnant Lucy Ricardo into the storyline of Ball's popular TV show.

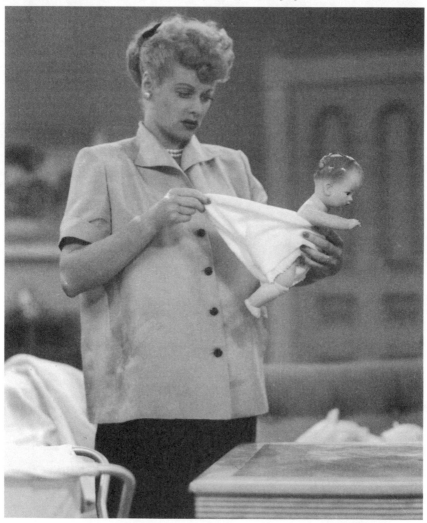

Many episodes of the show centered on Lucy's schemes to get into show business at the same time that Ricky was dead set against it. She continued to try, using a variety of disguises and ploys—as well as Ethel's help—and each attempt made Ricky more exasperated.

By every standard, the show was a triumph from its first episode. It became the first program ever to be seen in 10 million homes—out of a total of only 15 million television sets at the time. *I Love Lucy* became a Monday-night ritual, so important to viewers that in 1952 when presidential candidate Adlai Stevenson interrupted the show with a five-minute campaign message, his campaign office was besieged with hate mail.

Critics praised all of the actors, but Ball was the hands-down star. A reporter for *Time* magazine described her as "a redheaded, uninhibited comedienne who takes pratfalls and pie-throwing in her stride, manages to add on an extra wriggle or a rubber-faced double-take to each funny line." [32]

Accusations

When Ball became pregnant again, the network executives were not upset by the pregnancy, as Ball had worried that they might be; instead, the creative team wrote a pregnant Lucy Ricardo into the script. (The word "expecting" had to be used, because "pregnant" was considered too graphic for television in the 1950s.) With the birth of their real-life second child, Desi Jr., the future seemed bright.

However, the following year brought unforeseen trouble. The hearings of the House on Un-American Activities Committee (HUAC) accused Ball of being a Communist. In the early 1950s, many writers and actors were banned from working in Hollywood if they were known to be Communists. However, Ball had a ready explanation. Her grandfather had been a Socialist, and he had urged her to register as a Communist. She did so just to please her grandfather, she said, not because of any political thoughts of her own.

Despite headlines in a Los Angeles newspaper that proclaimed "Lucille Ball Named Red," [33] HUAC officially cleared her of any wrongdoing. However, both Ball and Arnaz were nervous that simply being questioned by HUAC might ruin her reputation and force the show to be canceled.

Before the next filming episode, Arnaz went out to talk to the audience. He made a short speech about his Cuban background, and how he and his family had been thrown out of Cuba for fighting the Communists:

> We hated them. They destroyed our lives and I wasn't about
> to marry one. During my years in the United States Army I

became a U.S. citizen, and one of the things I admire about this country is that you're innocent until proven guilty.

Up to now, you've only read what people have said about Lucy, but you have not had a chance to read our answer to those accusations. I assure you that the only thing red about my wife is her hair—and even that isn't real! [34]

Problems

The audience's response was supportive and warm, and Ball's future—as well as that of the show—seemed secure. Both she and Arnaz were collecting big salaries and were heads of a successful television production studio.

But the happy life of Lucy and Ricky Ricardo was far different from that of Lucille Ball and Desi Arnaz. Arnaz was drinking more and more, and there were rumors of him seeing other women. The added strain of the forced togetherness on the set each day made the marriage become unbearable.

In 1960, they did their final show together, and the following day, Ball filed for divorce. "It wasn't the industry and our working that broke us up," she later explained, "but the pressure had a lot to do with it. He was a very sick man. I was living with hope for many years. When the children got to an age when they were noticing the unhappiness, it was time to move away." [35]

A Busy Life

Just because *I Love Lucy* had ended, however, did not mean an end to Ball's career. To take her mind off the stresses of her personal life, she threw herself into other projects. She appeared with Bob Hope in the movie *The Facts of Life*, and then moved back to New York City with her children to begin rehearsing a Broadway musical called *Wildcat*.

The character she played on Broadway was a tomboyish oil prospector who arrives in the Old West with her disabled sister. Even though that didn't resemble her Lucy character in the least, audiences flocked to see her. The reviewers thought she did a good job, but they were less than impressed with the show as a whole. Wrote one, "It is good to see the handsome, talented, and vital Lucille Ball on the Broadway stage. It would be even better to see her in a good show." [36]

One positive thing to come from her time on Broadway was meeting Gary Morton, a nightclub comedian. Some friends of hers had thought the two might enjoy each other's company, and they were

Ball returned to television in 1962 with The Lucy Show, *playing a widow raising two young children.*

right. "Besides liking his looks," recalled Ball later, "I also liked his sense of humor. Before I met Gary, I hadn't laughed in years."[37] Morton and Ball were married on November 19, 1961.

Back to TV

After finishing her run on Broadway, Ball felt like returning to television. Desilu launched a new series in 1962, called *The Lucy Show*. In it, she would play Lucy Carmichael, a widow raising two young children. Ball was eager for Vivian Vance—who had played Ethel in *I*

Love Lucy—to play her divorced friend on the series. Vance agreed, and the show did well. In fact, it placed among the top ten-rated programs for its entire run until 1968. It was also the first television show that revolved around the lives of single women raising families.

Meanwhile, Arnaz had been president of Desilu but had decided to step down to pursue other interests. By that time, the production company had become enormously successful, with hits such as *The Andy Griffith Show, The Untouchables, The Dick Van Dyke Show,* and a host of others. Ball decided to buy her ex-husband's shares of Desilu, making her the company's sole owner. It was still another first for her—she became the first female president of a major Hollywood film company.

She did another series after that—*Here's Lucy,* which ran for another six years and which also starred her real-life daughter and son, Lucie Arnaz and Desi Arnaz Jr. When asked about the popularity of the Lucy character throughout the years, Ball explained that people liked the consistency. "People seem grateful that Lucy is there, the same character and unchanging view," she said. "There's so much chaos in the world, that's important." [38]

"She Was Loved"

But no matter how many movies or television shows Ball did, the role by which the public knew her was Lucy Ricardo. Nothing she had done before and nothing she did afterward received as much popularity.

Friends said that it was difficult for Ball to age, for the public had trouble seeing her as an older woman. She knew they wanted her to appear as she had in *I Love Lucy,* but that was almost impossible. Sometimes it seemed easier just to stay at home, as one of her friends confided. "She didn't like to go out because people didn't want to see the way she looked," she said. "When she did go out [in the evening], she spent the day with makeup people. She would do anything short of surgery to look good." [39]

Her final television appearance was a departure for her. She played a homeless woman in the 1986 made-for-television movie, *Stone Pillow.* She was pleased with the high praise her acting brought and toyed with the idea of making a comeback in her old Lucy character. But on April 26, 1986, while recovering from heart surgery, she unexpectedly died.

The news of her death shocked fans across the country. Lucille Ball was more than a comedian, she was a part of the American culture. Not only had she forged new territory by being the first woman to head a film studio, the popularity of *I Love Lucy* in the early days of television had shown how powerful that medium could be.

Ball made her last television appearance in the drama Stone Pillow, *playing an elderly homeless woman.*

The American public was saddened to learn of her death; it was the lead story in every news broadcast. In a statement that day, President George Bush said, "Lucille Ball possessed the gift of laughter. But she also embodied an even greater treasure—the gift of love. She appealed to the gentler impulses of the human spirit. She was not merely an actress or a comedian. She was 'Lucy,' and she was loved."[40]

CHAPTER 3

Whoopi Goldberg

In a 1984 interview, Whoopi Goldberg insisted that she did not think of herself as a true comedian, because she was not brave enough to do what comedians do. "The desperation that comes with being a stand-up comedian," she explained then, "is too frightening for me." [41] But looking at what she has accomplished in the years since that time in the field of comedy and acting, it is clear that while some things may frighten her, almost nothing stops her. Coming from the projects of New York City, Whoopi Goldberg has become a genuine superstar who has made a career of challenging herself—as well as her audiences—to listen as well as laugh.

Caryn

She was born on November 13, 1955, in New York City. Her name was Caryn Elaine Johnson—the name Whoopi Goldberg would come later. Goldberg likes to joke that her drive to perform began early in life—in fact, at birth:

> As soon as I popped into the birth room, I looked over in a corner, and there was my old man Destiny smilin' at me. My mother knew, too. She felt I was gonna be special. Different. From the very beginning, she knew. The story she tells was that I came out—headfirst, of course—pulled one arm through, looked around the delivery room, turned to the light, put my thumb in my mouth, and stared right back at all the folks who were staring at me. The spotlight was on me for the very first time, and I guess I thought it was kind of cool. [42]

Caryn was the second child born to Robert and Emma Johnson. Her brother, Clyde, was six years older. The family lived in a little sixth-floor apartment in a housing project in downtown Manhattan. Her neighborhood, called Chelsea, was a melting pot of many ethnic groups—Puerto Rican, Italian, Greek, and African.

Her parents' marriage was not a strong one, and soon after Caryn was born, Robert Johnson left his family. Emma, who had been working as a nurse, was forced to make some changes. Needing a job that allowed her more regular hours at home, she began teaching at Head Start and raising her two children alone.

"A Death-Ray Look That Could Melt Concrete"

Goldberg recalls her mother as being strict and very different from the mothers of her friends. Her mother did not need to yell or scold; both Caryn and her brother knew that there were limits to how naughty they could be. "[She was] a very formidable woman," Goldberg says. "Very. There wasn't a lot of testing the waters with her. She had a death-ray look that could melt concrete, that could burn through walls. She didn't have to say a word, nothing. Just the look could tear you apart." [43]

Unlike other black children in their neighborhood, Caryn and her brother were not allowed to use slang; they spoke with their mother's precise, cultured manner. "When people spoke to us," Goldberg remembers, "we spoke like this [using a very refined, well-modulated voice]. Kids would say, 'Wanna do sumpin?' and we'd say, 'No, thank you.'" [44]

Eventually, to feel more connected with other children, she learned to "double talk"—use fast slang with friends and more genteel language at home. As biographer James Robert Parish writes, "This ability to mimic and adapt her voice would prove to be very useful in later life." [45]

Happy Memories

Despite the fact that Emma was strict, her daughter has happy memories of her early years. The time spent playing outside was fun, for there was always something to do and plenty of children to play with. One of her

Despite growing up poor, Goldberg has fond memories of her childhood.

favorite times was after dinner, when the ice cream man came around.

> I'd yell up to our window, "Ma! Throw me a quarter!" and she'd stick her head out [the window of the apartment]. [W]e all called up, [and] you could see the curtains fluttering. It's like the whole building shook. Every parent knew their kid's call. You could call from across the street, and they'd know. They'd stick their heads out the windows and holler back, "Don't yell! Just come upstairs!"[46]

Sometimes the children would be excited to see the truck carrying sets and bleachers for Shakespeare in the Park, a group that brought Shakespearean theater to city neighborhoods. Caryn enjoyed that. "It was like the circus was coming to town," she remembers, "and on those nights our little neighborhood was the center of the . . . universe. The theater came to us. And it was free."[47]

School Problems

When Caryn was old enough to begin school, however, her life became much more difficult. She attended St. Columba, a Catholic grade school near her home. She was somewhat in awe of the nuns, who, because their long, black habits covered their feet, appeared to float down the halls.

Caryn tried to do the work expected of her, but had a difficult time. She was slow to learn and had a tendency to daydream. In those days teachers knew little about various learning disabilities; today she would have been diagnosed with dyslexia, a disorder that can affect memory, concentration, and reading.

Goldberg later conquered her disability. "I learned how to deal with dyslexia," she says, "through a lot of hard work and with the help of a lot of different people."[48] However, as an elementary school student at St. Columba School in the early 1960s, Caryn Johnson was thought by her teachers to be slow at best, and possibly even mentally retarded.

Refuge

School eroded her self-confidence, but Caryn had one activity that helped her escape the feelings of frustration: watching movies. When her mother had free time, she'd take her daughter to see current movies. But when that wasn't possible, Caryn watched old movies on television. She watched comedies, such as those starring Abbott and Costello or the Three Stooges, and laughed at the slapstick antics. Her favorites, however, were movies from the 1930s, 1940s, and 1950s, featuring glamorous stars such as Norma Shearer, Joan Crawford, Clark

As a young girl, Caryn enjoyed movies starring glamorous actresses such as Carole Lombard, pictured here in My Man Godfrey.

Gable, and John Garfield. It was an exciting world of make-believe, and, Goldberg recalls, it belonged to her:

> John Garfield . . . Honey, that man made me crazy as a kid. Just something about him. Or Carole Lombard. Goddess! When I saw Carole Lombard coming down some stairs in some long satin thing, I thought, I can do that. I wanted to come down those stairs, and say those words, and live that life. I knew it was all fantasy, but it seemed like so much fun. . . . You could do anything up there in the movies. You could fly. You could meet alien life forms. You could be a queen.[49]

"Anything Is Possible for You"

Emma Johnson knew how much her daughter enjoyed movies. She encouraged Caryn to experience even more than old movies; one of the most important gifts she gave her daughter was frequent exposure to the cultural events that were part of New York life. Plays, art exhibits, concerts—if she could find a way to get Caryn to such events, she did. But even more exciting to Caryn than seeing such things was doing them herself.

Caryn began attending the Hudson Guild, a community-based art center in her neighborhood. The Guild offered a range of after-school activities for children—acting programs, singing and juggling classes, storytimes, and much more. "For me it was like being in a candy store and being able to have any piece of candy I wanted," Goldberg now recalls. "I knew right away that I liked it." [50]

It was evident to those who were acquainted with young Caryn Johnson how much she liked it. One of her teachers at St. Columba recognized that performing was vital to the little girl. "The Hudson Guild was Caryn's first love," says Sister Jeanne Fielder. "Acting was in her genes. She was a performer. You couldn't miss it." [51]

Her mother, too, understood her daughter's love of make-believe and told her over and over that she could be a success if she worked at it hard enough. "My mother would tell me, 'I know you want to be a performer. Don't be afraid even if things don't work out the way you have them planned. Anything is possible for you.'" [52]

Quitting

The endless possibilities her mother talked about seemed far away when Caryn began high school, however. She had trouble with her classes; she found the work difficult and the teachers uncaring. But even more discouraging to Caryn was her lack of friends. She felt cut off from other students; her interests seemed strange to them, and, she recalls, she was not good at making friends:

> I was just not a popular girl. I couldn't get a boyfriend. I couldn't get into a clique. I felt I wasn't hip enough or smart enough or fast enough or funny enough or cute enough. I couldn't even dance well. . . . I wanted so much to be accepted that I'd hang out in the park with some of the girls and guys, and when they'd say, "Well, we want to get some candy," I'd run and I'd get some candy [for them]. But I'd come back and they'd have gone. And I'd sit and wait. [53]

Over her mother's objections, Caryn left school just a few weeks after she started high school. Though she continued to perform occasionally with the Hudson Guild, she participated in fewer and fewer organized activities. Instead, she roamed the city, taking part in much of what the youth culture of the 1960s offered. Some of her activities were ones she feels were very positive, such as taking part in civil rights or anti–Vietnam War demonstrations. Other activities, however, were more dangerous and would have life-changing consequences for the teenager.

The Lost Years

This is a time in her life, says Goldberg today, of which she is not proud. She refers to these years as her "lost years" because her life was out of her control. Her drug use was rampant; she used heroin,

LSD, uppers, downers, marijuana, and speed. "I did everything," she explains. "And large quantities of everything."[54]

She also engaged in a lot of unprotected sex; as a result, she became pregnant at age fourteen and again at age fifteen. Both pregnancies ended in abortion. Although she is open about many aspects of her past, Whoopi Goldberg does not like to give many details about this time in her life. "It's just something I don't want to talk about for public consumption, you know?. . . I just keep this stuff to myself. I lived. I survived. I grew up."[55]

A New Life

By the time she turned seventeen, Caryn knew that she could not continue her street life. She was homeless and uneducated. She was addicted to drugs. Her world, she says, "had started getting real dark real fast."[56] She checked herself into a haven for addicts called Horizon House, and worked hard to get clean and sober.

When Caryn left Horizon House, she was determined to start on a better path. Worrying that she might be tempted to go back to drugs, she agreed to marry Alvin Martin, one of her drug counselors. She knows now that it was a foolish reason to get married, for they had little in common. Alvin was steady, responsible, and by-the-rules; she was his direct opposite. She wanted to find a way to return to her acting; he wanted her to get a safer job with a steady income.

After completing treatment for drug abuse, Caryn was determined to pursue an acting career.

One thing they *did* have in common, however, was a baby daughter—Alexandrea—born when Caryn was eighteen. But the marriage was doomed to fail. Said Alvin later, "She wanted to be a movie star, and I wanted to pay bills. The two things don't mix."[57] The couple split up after two years of marriage, and Caryn and Alexandrea moved back in with Emma.

But she stayed only three weeks. A friend was going to the West Coast and was willing to take Caryn and her baby along. Excited that this might be the impetus to her acting career, she eagerly accepted. And even though her

Goldberg, after a performance of her one-woman show in 1984.

friend decided not to go all the way to Los Angeles, the heart of the film industry, instead settling in San Diego, Caryn remained optimistic. It would be the start of a new life for her and her daughter.

A New Name

Acting opportunities were difficult to get in San Diego, however. Caryn auditioned for roles in anything—dinner theater, repertory theater, even comedy groups. During this time she realized how few roles there were for black people. Since whites made up the majority of theatergoers at the time, theater owners were reluctant to put on plays with interracial story lines. If a person of color was included in a cast, it was usually to play a maid, servant, or criminal.

Caryn was also beginning to realize how different her looks were from those of most successful actresses. She had never been considered pretty; her wide grin, prominent nose, and dreadlocks were definitely not dainty or beguiling—two traits that many casting directors sought in their female stars. Even so, she persisted in making the rounds, talking to directors, and hoping for a big break.

While Caryn was reluctant to change herself too much to land a part, she did decide to change her name. As she recalls, she and some other actress friends were thinking about unusual names for children. One young woman told Caryn that her mother should have named her Whoopi, since she had problems with intestinal gas and therefore sounded at times like a whoopee cushion. The other women laughed, and so did Caryn.

She decided at first to change her name to Whoopi Cushion; however, her mother objected. Emma told her daughter that while casting directors might remember the name, they would never take her seriously as an actress. Caryn compromised, keeping Whoopi and using the name Goldberg, after a distant relative. From then on, she was Whoopi Goldberg, except to her family members, who still call her Caryn.

Part-Time Welfare Mother

While Goldberg was able to find a few jobs performing, they paid next to nothing. She didn't care, however, for she was doing what she loved and was learning each day. But paying the bills, especially with a baby daughter, was important, too. She needed jobs besides acting to pay rent and buy groceries.

She held a variety of jobs during her early years as an actress—everything from a bank teller to a bricklayer. She even worked in a mortuary as a cosmetician, helping to prepare the bodies for funerals. When even those jobs weren't enough, she went on welfare—an experience she still remembers with discomfort.

A few years later, after she had begun making enough money to support herself and Alexandrea, Goldberg says that it was a wonderful feeling. "The greatest thing I ever was able to do," she says, "was give a welfare check back. I brought it back to the welfare department and said, 'Here, I don't need this anymore.'" [58]

To Berkeley and The Spook Show

One type of performance that Goldberg was starting to love was improvisational comedy, in which actors made up the story as they went along. She was a part of an improvisational group in San Diego called Spontaneous Combustion, and soon found herself learning a comedian's most important tool—to think fast on her feet. In 1980, she decided to move to Berkeley, a suburb of San Francisco, to join an improvisational group there, called the Blake Street Hawkeyes.

With the Hawkeyes, Goldberg honed her acting and comedy skills even more. She also developed her own one-woman show, which she called *The Spook Show*—a title that offended some black people. "Spook," they reminded her, had long been used as a derogatory term for a black person. However, she explained that she was using the word to refer to the inner spirits or life forces that inhabit *all* people and make each person an individual.

The show was made up of a number of characters Goldberg had created—some male, some female, and from a variety of ethnic backgrounds. She became Fontaine, the street-smart thief with a drug problem, as well as a teenage Valley Girl who just found out she was pregnant. She was a young handicapped woman and an elderly Jamaican. Probably her most endearing character was a nine-year-old black girl who wanted to be white.

The skits were funny, but they also made audiences think. The little nine-year-old got laughs as she shyly talked about herself, but when she confided that she bathed in bleach to become whiter, the audience would gasp. Goldberg engaged her audiences with quick ad

49

libs, drawing on her improvisational background. Her ability to use various dialects and costumes made people see her characters rather than Whoopi Goldberg.

Success

While *The Spook Show* did not start out strong, word soon spread about this unusual woman and her exotic collection of characters. Critics were generally positive about the show; one called Goldberg "a fresh and very funny character comedian with a distinctive point of view and rich comic potential . . . not simply a stand-up comedian but a satirist with a cutting edge." [59]

One man who enjoyed her show was Mike Nichols, a longtime comedian himself, who had begun directing and producing. Nichols believed Goldberg's show would do well on Broadway and talked her into relocating to New York. He helped her polish her act, and to eliminate the misunderstanding about the term "spook" in the title, he changed the name of the show to *Whoopi Goldberg: Direct from Broadway.*

The show ran for 150 performances, from October 1984 to March 1985, and attracted large audiences. Some criticized the show as disjointed or too sentimental. But few could argue that Goldberg had a gift for comedy that indicated she would have a bright future in show business. Though *Whoopi Goldberg: Direct from Broadway* did not win its star a Tony (the highest honor for a stage actor), the soundtrack to the show did win a Grammy Award.

The Color Purple

One of Goldberg's new fans was director Steven Spielberg, who had had one huge Hollywood hit after another—from *Jaws* to *E.T.*, to *Raiders of the Lost Ark* and its sequel, *Indiana Jones and the Temple of Doom.* Spielberg was casting for a new movie based on a novel by Alice Walker. Called *The Color Purple,* the book centers on Celie, an abused young woman who gradually discovers the strength within herself. After seeing Goldberg's one-woman show, Spielberg thought she might be a good choice for Celie.

The book was not new to Goldberg. She had first heard of it in 1983, when she and Alexandrea were driving around Berkeley; Alice Walker was on the radio reading selections from the book. Goldberg remembers one selection featured two characters who were talking about God. She says that Alexandrea "had made me pull over, because I talk about God a lot, and she thought it was funny that somebody else was saying the same kind of stuff. So," Goldberg said, "I knew I had to read it." [60]

She was glad she did; the story moved her enormously. She even wrote to Walker, begging the author to consider her for any part should the book ever be made into a movie. "I'd be dirt on the floor,"[61] she pleaded. When Spielberg offered her the leading role years later, she was in heaven. "My teeth caught cold," she remembers, "cause all I could do was grin."[62]

Arriving

Her performance in *The Color Purple* firmly established Goldberg as a major talent. She was nominated for an Academy Award and won a Golden Globe for her work; casting director Reuben Cannon said she was "the closest thing to genius I've ever seen."[63]

Suddenly Whoopi Goldberg was one of the most sought-after stars in show business. She was a guest on *Saturday Night Live*, she was named one of *People* magazine's "Twenty-five Most Intriguing People of the Year," and she was the first black woman ever to receive the Female Star of the Year Award in Las Vegas. Her family was proud of her, and for the first time in her life, she felt as if she had enough money to splurge a little.

Goldberg's portrayal of Celie in The Color Purple *earned her an Academy Award nomination.*

Asked when she realized that she had truly arrived in show business, Goldberg said, "I don't know. But I do remember I bought my kid three pairs of shoes. . . . And afterward, she wore mismatched shoes because she was so proud to have more than one pair." [64]

Grandma Whoopi

But the next few years would see some disappointments, too. Her longtime relationship with David Schein, who had worked with her in Berkeley, had deteriorated. This was hard on Alexandrea, too, for Schein had taken over some of the parenting in California while Goldberg was appearing on Broadway.

Her relationship troubles continued. While filming a documentary on the homeless in 1986, she met a Dutch filmmaker named David Claessen. The two married the same year, but the marriage failed less than two years later.

Family troubles arose as well. Fourteen-year-old Alexandrea shocked Goldberg in 1989 when she announced that she was pregnant. Long a champion of the pro-choice cause, Goldberg was surprised that her daughter was insistent on having the baby. Goldberg supported her daughter's decision, however, and was proud when her granddaughter, Amarah, was born on her grandmother's thirty-fourth birthday. "Now," announced the comedian, "I'm Grandma Whoopi." [65]

Busy

For years after her film debut in *The Color Purple*, Goldberg continued to make movies, including *Burglar* (1987), *Clara's Heart* (1988), and *Kiss Shot* (1989). She accepted roles that she found interesting and that she thought might help her improve as an actor. But these films were average at best, and the critics were not kind.

She persevered, however, doing television appearances in series such as *Moonlighting* with Bruce Willis and Cybill Shepherd, and *Star Trek: The Next Generation*. She teamed with fellow comics Billy Crystal and Robin Williams in a fund-raiser for the homeless in Los Angeles. Called Comic Relief, the program raised more than $2 million and was so entertaining that it became a yearly charity event. She was busy, but she felt as though she was not living up to other people's expectations since *The Color Purple*.

But in 1990 everything changed. A new movie was being cast, called *Ghost*. One part was especially interesting to Goldberg: the role of Oda Mae Brown, a con artist and psychic. But the director did not want someone as well known as Whoopi Goldberg for the role, so she was rejected. However, the star of the movie, Patrick Swayze, was an admirer of her work and urged the director to reconsider. In July

1989, Goldberg was offered the part of the quirky con artist, in what would become the smash hit movie of the summer of 1990.

An Oscar and More Success

Goldberg won an Oscar for her performance and was thrilled. She charmed reporters who later asked how it felt to have won. "Baby," she grinned, "I was so happy. It was—it's one of those moments that you can never, ever. . . . There's not enough time in the world to explain what happened. But I wanted that so badly, and for all my life." [66]

Her success with *Ghost* was followed by *Sister Act,* a comedy about a singer hiding from the mob in a convent. It was so successful, she was immediately hired to do a sequel, *Sister Act 2: Back in the Habit.* She continued her work with Comic

Goldberg won an Oscar for her 1990 performance in Ghost.

Relief and tackled a host of new projects—doing the voice of Shenzi the Hyena for *The Lion King,* playing the wife of slain civil rights activist Medgar Evers in *Ghosts of Mississippi,* and hosting her own talk show.

Breaking New Ground

She continued to break new ground, too. Hoping to return to Broadway, she went after the lead in the successful comedy *A Funny Thing Happened on the Way to the Forum.* Interestingly, the role was Plautus, which had been played only by white men—the latest being Nathan Lane.

But Lane was leaving, and Goldberg thought it would be fun to try it for a limited run. She got the part, and New York audiences loved her. One critic wrote that she "has marked her claim to the territory . . . like a cat taking over a chair in an unfamiliar apartment." [67]

Another groundbreaker was doing a film called *Sarafina!*, which was set in South Africa. That nation had long had a system of legalized segregation, and Goldberg was the first black female actress from the United States ever to do a film in that country.

An Honest Look

Whoopi Goldberg has accomplished a great deal as a comedian and as an actor, and she continues to work on new projects. Her friends say that her risk taking has allowed her to expand her talents in many areas. She may succeed or she may fail, but she will learn something in the process.

She continues to be outspoken on things she believes in, too. For instance, using the term "black" rather than "African American" is considered by some people to be politically incorrect. But Goldberg is adamant that she is not African American. "I've been criticized by the black community, and loudly," she admits. "But I'm a fifth- or sixth-generation American, and I also have Chinese and white in me. . . . I'm not culturally from Africa. I've been in Africa—I know better." [68]

Whoopi Goldberg is a woman who is difficult to label—either in her work or in her personal life. Perhaps that is the key to her enormous success and her transformation from high school dropout, drug addict, and teenage welfare mother to the funny and talented woman she has become.

CHAPTER 4

Roseanne

Audiences knew her first as Roseanne Barr and then as Roseanne Arnold. Today she is one of a handful of celebrities for whom one name is enough: Roseanne. Her nasal, whiny voice is instantly recognizable, as is her roly-poly physique. She is loud, opinionated, and unafraid of what anyone—man or woman—thinks of her. She complains about her children, her husband, and trying to clean her house. "The day I worry about cleaning my house," she says, "is the day that Sears comes out with a riding vacuum cleaner." [69]

Roseanne Barr overcame poverty and childhood abuse to become one of America's most well known comedians.

The great success she has achieved may be surprising to many; Roseanne is quite the opposite of the pleasant, demure, model-thin women who have long been typical Hollywood types. But her success is far more amazing in light of the intense struggles she has gone through to get there—poverty, physical problems, as well as sexual and emotional abuse, as she revealed in 1991. She is, marvels one reporter, "one of the great improbables of the late-twentieth century." [70]

Growing Up Poor

Roseanne Barr was born in Salt Lake City, Utah, on November 3, 1953—the first child of Helen and Jerry Barr. The Barrs were Jewish, which made them part of a tiny minority in Salt Lake City, which was mostly Mormon. Jerry worked sporadically; he had neither the ambition nor the educational background to get a well-paying job.

One of his more interesting jobs was being a door-to-door sales-man with his father, Roseanne's Grandpa Sam. Occasionally he sold vacuum cleaners, curtains, and a variety of products aimed at the rather small Catholic population of Salt Lake City. "He sold cruci-fixes and 3-D pictures of Jesus door to door," remembers Roseanne. "Our house was full of them. You'd walk by and Jesus would blink or his hands would spread out." [71]

Helen, who was barely nineteen when her oldest daughter was born, baby-sat occasionally to earn money. She also kept the books for Sam and Jerry's sales. Neither job brought much income to the family, and most of her time was spent caring for Roseanne and three younger children, Geraldine, Ben, and Stephanie. With little money and no prospects, the Barr family seemed destined for a life of poverty.

Outsider

Roseanne was an outsider as a child; in fact, she says that from the time she was very young, comedy has been her way of escaping the hurt feelings she experienced. Being Jewish, for example, set her apart from her peers. In elementary school she was one of a hand-ful of non-Mormons, and she was singled out frequently by teach-ers. "At every Christmas pageant," Roseanne recalls, "the teachers would say, 'And now our little Jewish girl, Roseanne Barr, will sing a song about a dreidel [a toy used at Hanukkah celebrations].' So I would sing the dreidel song, and then explain why I didn't believe in Jesus." [72]

But religion was not the only reason she felt alone. She was chunky—perhaps twenty pounds overweight. "An adult would see her as a healthy, normal child," her sister Geraldine remembers. "Yet to kids, Rosey was fat, so Rosey was taunted." [73] Geraldine recalls one year in grade school when Roseanne's class was doing a physical fit-ness test.

Each child would take a turn running one hundred yards while the rest of the class watched and the teacher kept time with a stopwatch. The weekend before her turn at running, Roseanne was terrified, even begging her younger sister to jump on her leg to break it. (Though she was reluctant, Geraldine agreed to try by jumping on Roseanne's leg, but succeeded only in bruising it.)

An Unpredictable Family

Roseanne might have found it difficult to fit in socially simply because her family was unusual. Roseanne says that her father spent a great deal of time lying on the sofa watching television. He bathed and changed his clothes only a couple of times a month, especially during those periods when he was unemployed, and insisted that his daughters wait on him. Once, she says, he even called her at a friend's house, telling her to come home to change the channel for him.

Both Helen and Jerry had explosive tempers as well. Geraldine Barr writes, "I have memories of each of [our parents], pushed to the limit, becoming overly physical in anger when one or another of us children did something wrong."[74]

Helen's temper could take a strange twist, however, when directed at anyone who dared threaten or taunt one of her children. When Roseanne was little, a neighborhood boy made fun of her, calling her fatso. Helen urged her daughter to invite him over for a piece of chocolate cake, and she would teach the boy how to be nice. Helen called out from inside the house, asking if he would like a piece of cake. Roseanne remembers:

> She had already smeared this purple facial mask on her face, and as it dried, it drew her face taut, making her eyes look very bloodshot and her lips very swollen. She took out her false teeth, and smeared ketchup all over her hands and mouth and neck . . . and she came out, holding a piece of cake, covered with about one and one-half bottles of ketchup. "Here, Curtis," she said, real slow, "here's your cake." I'll never forget that kid's face.[75]

Bobbe Mary

The adult Roseanne was closest to was her maternal grandmother, Mary Davis, known to Roseanne and her siblings as Bobbe Mary (*bobbe* is the Yiddish word for "grandmother"). Bobbe Mary had grown up in Eastern Europe, but because of the massacres and other atrocities aimed at Jews, her father had sent her and an older sister to the United States when she was sixteen. He had hoped to save enough to send his other eight children, but it did not happen in time—they were all killed by the Nazis during World War II.

Bobbe Mary owned an apartment building in Salt Lake City, which she managed after her husband died. Many of her tenants were Holocaust survivors, says Roseanne, and Mary was generous and supportive to them. Roseanne spent a great deal of her childhood in Bobbe Mary's apartment, playing gin rummy, eating, and talking.

Mary Davis was strong and cynical—two qualities that Roseanne admired. "I loved my grandmother more than any other human being," says Roseanne, "because she never lied, never told you what you wanted to hear, never compromised."[76]

Born to Entertain

Roseanne's talent for entertaining might have come from her grandmother as well. Davis had dreamed of a career in show business when she first came to the United States. She was an accomplished singer and encouraged Roseanne to have high goals, too.

Roseanne enjoyed entertaining at a young age. She danced and sang, holding a screwdriver as though it were a microphone, while she imitated singers she knew from the radio or television. She also organized large-scale "shows," using her siblings and children in the neighborhood. One act consisted of two neighbor boys who ran into each other and butted heads. Another boy who was born with a genetic defect—webbing between his toes—took off his shoes and socks (accompanied by two boys doing a drumroll on the kitchen table with their hands) and displayed the webbing. But the star of the show was always Roseanne; she sang the opening number, the closing number, and several tunes in the middle.

"Comedian, Comedian!"

Her love of comedy came from her father, who would yell, "Comedian, comedian!" whenever a good comic would appear on one of the television shows he watched. He pointed out the good ones to his children and loudly criticized the ones who had nothing to say. Roseanne remembers enjoying a variety of comedians, such as Lucille Ball, Jackie Vernon, Moms Mabley, and Phyllis Diller.

Her father explained to her that comedy was at its absolute funniest when it was used by minorities or "the little man" against the powerful. He also taught her that some of the best comedy was aimed at long-established traditions, those things commonly called "sacred cows." Humor was a way of putting people on equal footing.

As Roseanne grew, she found that she had a knack for quick one-liners like the comedians she saw on television. At thirteen and fourteen she was smart and could think on her feet—two necessities for any comedian. She recalls that she and her father would sometimes have head-to-head comedy battles, in which he would say something critical of women, and she would counter with a joke about him:

> We would have contests and showdowns and I would always win. My father taught me that comedy is mightier than the sword and the pen. And even though he was a sexist pig, if I would say something that was very anti-male, or anti-him, and it was funny, my father would applaud and say "good one." [77]

The Accident

The defining moment of Roseanne's young life, however, was not funny in the least. It happened during her sophomore year, when she and her friend Sherri were on their way to school. The girls were walking diagonally across the street, when Roseanne was hit by a car; the driver had been momentarily blinded by the bright sun.

Roseanne was hit so hard that the car's hood ornament opened a large gash on her head. She was

A near-fatal accident during Roseanne's sophomore year changed her outlook on life.

comatose for a time, and when she finally awoke, her frightened family was ecstatic. But as they would soon learn, it was a different Roseanne who emerged after that accident. The experience had been a turning point in her life, one that greatly affected how she would live from that point on.

Roseanne vividly remembers the changes that occurred afterward. She had trouble focusing in school, and her memory was poor. Once an A student, she struggled in her classwork. She also was plagued by odd dreams. "I would dream that I could not wake up," she says. "I was in bed trying to move even an eyelid, screaming at my paralyzed body to open its eyes. I was horrified that people would think I was dead and bury me alive." [78]

A Troubled Time

Roseanne's behavior changed drastically, too. She became wilder, misbehaving in school and at home. She began using marijuana and lying to her parents, who were baffled. After taking the family car without permission and getting in an accident, she was arrested and taken to juvenile hall.

Helen Barr was convinced that the accident had caused brain damage and that was the root of Roseanne's misbehavior. However, the doctors said no. She was healing, and there were no physical reasons to explain her actions. But Roseanne says now that the accident changed the way she looked at life. Being struck and almost killed taught her that she was mortal—a concept most teens don't think much about. And since her time on earth was limited, she was not going to be timid and conservative, writes her sister Geraldine:

> She no longer wanted to be a good girl. She no longer wanted to abstain from sensual experiences to win the favor of her Mormon friends. She wanted to drink coffee, smoke pot, lose her virginity, and wear the wild hippie clothing then in style. . . . She wanted to flee the strictures of Salt Lake City and discover all aspects of life that she could imagine trying. [79]

Gone

Roseanne agreed to counseling for a while, but when she made little progress, she checked herself into the state mental hospital in Provo— or as she calls it today, "the laughing academy." She does not talk much about her experiences there during her nine-month stay, except that the medications helped her get some much-needed sleep. She came home occasionally on weekends but continued her rebellious ways.

She became pregnant during one weekend, and a few months later, told her parents. They were angry and disappointed, and Roseanne ran away to a Salvation Army home for unwed mothers in Denver. On May 16, 1971, she gave birth to a girl, who was adopted just days later by a Denver couple. Still bitter over her hospitalization and her parents' lack of support during her pregnancy, Roseanne did not want to return to Utah. Her new life, she decided, would be in Colorado.

Married

Roseanne had a friend, Linda, who was living in a commune in Georgetown, a small town in the mountains above Denver. Linda urged her to move there, insisting that the life they lived would be perfect for Roseanne. After a sixteen-hour bus ride, Roseanne was on her own in Colorado.

Not long after arriving, she went into a motel lobby and asked to use the bathroom. The clerk on duty was Bill Pentland, a man who would soon become her husband. Pentland was far different from men she had known before. He wrote poetry, was a storyteller, and was convinced that aliens were taking over the planet. He was a former user of LSD and suffered occasional flashbacks from previous drug use.

Even so, says Roseanne, it was love at first sight. They bought a trailer, got married, and moved to Manitou Springs, a suburb of Colorado Springs. Within three years, Roseanne had three children: Jessica, Jennifer, and Jacob. Bill worked at the post office, and she stayed at home with the children.

Isolated

But while she loved her children, Roseanne found that she was bored living in the trailer park, so far from friends. Bill was often distant, and she was lonely for someone to talk to. She tried making friends with women in the area, but they seemed confused when she would tell them that she wanted to write stories or poems. "These other women would look at me," recalls Roseanne, "like there was something wrong with me for wanting that, for saying that, for thinking about anything besides kids and dinner and husbands." [80]

She withdrew into herself, feeling isolated and different from other women. Because food was an easy companion, her weight soared. Her relationship with Bill soured; she discovered that he had been having an affair with another woman, and she became more depressed.

Roseanne began to feel isolated and depressed during her marriage to her first husband, Bill Pentland.

She became interested in the feminist movement in the early 1980s and worked at a Denver bookstore called Woman to Woman. Fascinated by the number of books about women's issues, Roseanne felt that she had found a niche with women like her who wanted more out of life than they had. During this time she read, wrote, and dieted, going from 200 pounds down to 105.

"Let's Go to Rosie's"

But while she was at first excited about feminism, she became annoyed with feminist leaders. They gave the impression of being committed to helping women, yet in reality they seemed uninterested in women like Roseanne, who were poor, working-class women. She made the decision to get a different job—first as a cocktail waitress and later, she hoped, as a writer. She began working in a bar called Bennigan's in Denver. It was there she realized what she was born to be: a comedian.

The customers—almost all men—began making comments and flirting in what she knew was a sexist manner. She let their comments go by, although inside she was angry. Finally, she says, one day she just snapped. "This man said, 'Bring me one of these, honey.' I turned around and I said, 'Don't call me honey, you [expletive] pig.'" [81]

Much to her surprise, the man started laughing, and she did, too. Realizing that she could spar with the customers and get laughs—much as she had done when she and her father had one-upped each other back in Salt Lake City—was exhilarating. Soon, men began needling her more frequently, waiting for her funny comebacks. The job became exciting after that; she looked forward to going to work and even thought about funny lines she could use in the future.

Her customers were loyal and supportive. "They would tell me that after they got off from work, they would never say, 'Let's go to Bennigan's,'" says Roseanne, "they would say, 'Let's go to Rosie's.' And I said, 'That is really cool.' And one man said, 'This is just like going to the Comedy Works, coming to see you, except that it lasts about six hours.'" [82] Roseanne had not heard of the Comedy Works, but she knew then and there that she was ready to see what stand-up comedy was all about.

Learning How

In August 1981, Roseanne became brave enough to visit a Denver comedy club. It was Monday, open mike night, when anyone could have a turn in front of the audience. To her amazement, her five-minute monologue did very well; some of the regulars at Bennigan's had come to cheer her on, and they were proud of her. She continued to show up

Roseanne honed her comedic skills by performing her stand-up routine at any opportunity.

every Monday and deliver whatever thoughts she'd had that week. However, she wanted to work more at the comedy club, working on days other than Mondays—and she wanted to get paid, too.

She performed at other places in town—a bookstore, a café that catered to bikers, and a coffeehouse in a church basement. She learned each time she went onstage, perfecting her timing, her mannerisms, and even her facial expressions. Her sister Geraldine, who had moved to Denver, was extremely supportive; she and Roseanne bounced ideas back and forth, many of them drawn from their past in conservative Salt Lake City. Even though they still had marital problems, Bill helped Roseanne with her act, too—coming up with ideas based on married life with three children.

With Geraldine urging her on, Roseanne took her show on the road. She appeared in clubs in a number of cities, from Kansas City and Louisville to San Francisco and, finally, Los Angeles. At that time, Mitzi Shore's Comedy Store was a venue that could make or break a comedian. Shore loved Roseanne's act, as did a member of the audience named Jim McCawley, talent director for *The Tonight Show,* starring Johnny Carson. McCawley's presence that night in 1987 was Roseanne's first big break.

Rising Star

McCawley offered Roseanne the opportunity that every comedian dreams about: to appear on Carson's top-rated show. Carson was very selective about the comedians he invited, and Roseanne knew it. She was giddy with excitement; her family back in Salt Lake City was joyous, too. Her brother Ben brought Bobbe Mary's diamond ring (Mary had died in 1981) so Roseanne could wear it on the show for luck.

She did well on *The Tonight Show*. Audiences who had not seen her act laughed as she talked about things that most comedians could not—simply because they were believable in *her* life:

> I figure when my husband comes home at night, if those kids are still alive, hey, I've done my job.

> Being a mom is rewarding. You've got all these little people and you could really mess up their heads forever. Only moms can say stuff like, "Don't talk with your mouth full. Answer me!"

> I'm on the mirror diet. You eat all your food in front of a mirror in the nude. It works pretty good, though some of the fancier restaurants don't go for it. [83]

After her appearance on *The Tonight Show*, Roseanne was flooded with bookings. Clubs around the country were eager to headline this heavy, whiny-voiced woman who could say almost anything as long as she smiled. She moved with Geraldine to Hollywood, and soon afterward Bill and her three children came out. She was interviewed by magazines and newspapers, and was offered an HBO special of her own. By the end of 1987, Roseanne was probably the most well known comic in the country.

Roseanne: Getting It Right

In 1988, Roseanne signed on to do a sitcom based on the material in her comedy act. The ABC network agreed to purchase a pilot and six episodes of the show, which was yet unnamed. A former writer on *The Cosby Show*, Matt Williams, had been hired to develop the idea for the show. However, he and Roseanne began bickering almost immediately.

The problem, it seemed, was that the production company had told Roseanne that she was the head writer; unfortunately, they had told Williams that *he* was the head writer. The two tried to collaborate on a first script, but when Roseanne saw Williams's final version, she was furious. Recalls Roseanne:

> When I read it and my God, I just flipped. . . . My character was totally passive, like just about every other woman on TV. Functionally, I may as well have been a pin-setter [before electric pin-

setters, a worker at a bowling alley who set up the pins before each ball was thrown] or the lady who hands the knife thrower his daggers. My character spent most of her time sitting in the corner like a stump, saying "And then what happened? And then what happened?" [84]

Roseanne had been told that her character—the main character—would, in fact, be a strong, funny woman. But although Williams rewrote the script several times, he never put Roseanne's character in the center. His versions featured the husband or the son as the pivotal character. "He couldn't understand," says Roseanne, "that the female character could *drive* scenes, that the family functioned *because* of her, not in spite of her." [85]

A Battle Won, and Acclaim

Roseanne ended up writing the pilot herself. And even though the hostility between her and Williams had been difficult, the end result was very good. The character of Roseanne was much like the real-life Roseanne—opinionated, brash, and funny. Her TV family, the Conners, were blue-collar people who struggled with real issues. Money

Roseanne was a hit with critics and television viewers, who enjoyed the cast's portrayal of a blue-collar family.

was frequently scarce, and their children—unlike children in many sitcoms—often misbehaved. And unlike many parents in sitcoms, Roseanne and her husband (played by John Goodman) could be impatient and short.

In one episode, for example, the children are whining and unpleasant because they are not getting their way. They ask Roseanne, "Why are you so mean?" "Because I hate kids," she snaps. "And I'm not your real mom." [86]

Critics were impressed with the show, and viewers were delighted. Letters poured in to ABC, congratulating the network for having the sense to portray a real family on television for once. *Roseanne* would run for a remarkable nine seasons—almost unheard of in television today.

Personal Troubles

But while Roseanne was having success with her television show, her private life was in disarray. She and her husband, Bill Pentland, did not get along. She claimed that he went behind her back, talking with Matt Williams during difficulties on the set and betraying her. She also accused him of selling stories about her to the supermarket tabloids.

As their relationship grew rancorous, she had become involved with a comedian named Tom Arnold. She had known Arnold since

Roseanne and comedian Tom Arnold created tabloid news with their public antics and outrageous behavior.

1983, when they were both doing stand-up. Although the two had become good friends, they had never been romantically linked. But in 1989, he told her he loved her. If she and Pentland would get a divorce, he promised, he would marry her. She agreed, and filed for divorce.

The new relationship had problems, however. Arnold was a cocaine addict; he had also fed tabloid reporters stories about his famous fiancée. For example, stories about the baby she had placed for adoption when she was a teenager were leaked, which she found especially disturbing.

Roseanne, furious that he was betraying her trust, first broke off the engagement. However, Arnold went into a drug treatment program and underwent counseling for various emotional problems, and he and Roseanne reconciled. The two were married on January 20, 1990.

Living in a Fishbowl

But Roseanne's problems continued, and because of her star status, they became fodder for gossip columnists. For instance, her relationship with her sister Geraldine was much talked about when Roseanne fired her sister from the *Roseanne* show in 1990. Geraldine had been a key force in Roseanne's comedy career all along, and to be dismissed was hurtful. (Geraldine's subsequent lawsuit against Roseanne for $70 million was well publicized, but was thrown out of court.)

Roseanne's marriage was a constant media circus as well. Arnold, who had been involved in the show as a writer, and then as a cast member, seemed to enjoy the publicity that accompanied them. In fact, many believe that the two enjoyed being as silly and outrageous as possible, for it kept their image in the public eye.

Roseanne made deadly serious headlines of her own in 1991 when she publicly announced on television that she had been sexually abused as a child. She had repressed the memories, she explained, but when husband Tom Arnold was going through therapy for drug addiction, his memories of abuse triggered her own. Though her parents deny abusing their daughter, Roseanne maintained that the abuse has caused lifelong trauma. "It's the secret that's been killing me my whole life," she said. "I feel like screaming; I feel like running; I struggle hard not to forget again." [87]

Two People—or More?

Her name has been in so many headlines, for so many different things, that it is difficult to keep Roseanne the person separate from Roseanne

Roseanne married her former body-guard, Ben Thomas, in 1995.

the comic. Her public antics, such as her divorce from Tom Arnold and subsequent marriage to her former bodyguard, Ben Thomas, have kept the tabloids busy.

Some have said she doesn't know when to keep her mouth shut. Others have defended her, saying that she's the honest breath of fresh air that Hollywood needs. But there have been few disagreements about her value to comedy and the impact she has had on its stereotypes.

Roseanne was not the first to talk about women's issues in her comedy act; however, she was the first to give American television audiences a new version of a family comedy. Rising from a poor, dysfunctional family herself, she was determined to show a slice of family life that was both real and funny; her stubborn refusal to allow the network executives to soften or temper that reality resulted in groundbreaking television.

CHAPTER 5

Ellen DeGeneres

For years Ellen DeGeneres was well known for her understated quips and the earnest manner she presented in her comedy acts. DeGeneres, who starred in her own television sitcom, *Ellen*, achieved a great deal of publicity when her TV character Ellen came out as a lesbian in a 1997 episode. DeGeneres herself is gay, but until that episode did not choose to make her sexuality public.

DeGeneres found herself the topic of lively debates after the show aired. Some called her brave and commended her for her honesty. Some applauded her as being a pioneer for gay people on television. Others, such as right-wing religious leader Jerry Falwell, dubbed her "Ellen Degenerate" [88] and used her as another example of the crumbling morality shown on television. Through it all, the comedy of the blond, blue-eyed DeGeneres remained the same—low-key and droll.

Roots

DeGeneres was born on January 26, 1958, in a suburb of New Orleans called Metairie. Her mother, Betty, was an administrative assistant at Newcomb College. Her father, Elliott, was an insurance salesman. Ellen was their second child; they had a son, Vance, who was four years older.

Her marriage to Elliott was Betty's second. She had been married at age seventeen to a young military man who was living on a base in another state. Seeing one another so rarely was not a good way to begin a marriage, Betty said later, and the two officially separated after being married less than a year.

Ellen DeGeneres rose to fame with her understated, observational humor.

Elliott DeGeneres was a quiet, kind man and a Christian Scientist. (That religion is founded on the idea that diseases should be cured by prayer and faith, not medicine or medical care.) Betty was impressed with his steadiness and reliability—especially after being married to a man who was never around. Ellen agrees that her father was always a calming presence in her life. "My father is very religious, very honest," she says. "My entire life, he's never raised his voice, never once." [89]

"No Different from the Rest"

Many comedians recall that they were funny early in life, and that their families knew that show business would be their future. But Ellen was not a little girl who liked the spotlight. One woman who went to school with Ellen says that she was just like everyone else.

"She wasn't a show-off or a class clown or even all that funny," she remembers. "La Salle was a small neighborhood school, the kind of place where everybody knows everybody. We'd go over to each other's house for birthday parties or to play, and Ellen's family was no different from the rest. There was nothing that made them stand out in your memory." [90]

DeGeneres remembers being more in awe of naturalists such as Jane Goodall and Dian Fossey than TV comedians. She loved animals and talked of being a veterinarian or a world traveler, to study apes. She set up a little office in the basement of her house, where she would fill notebooks with information on various types of cats, which she copied from the encyclopedia. She even claims to have given mouth-to-mouth resuscitation to a bird after it flew into a plate glass window.

Moving

Ellen's family moved quite often because of her father's work. Even though the moves were not long-distance ones, they were still difficult for Ellen and Vance. Each move meant a new school, a new neighborhood around New Orleans, and the need to make friends all over again.

She says now that moving so often made her extremely anxious to connect, to be liked. "It was weird being the new kid in school all the time, so I wanted to feel like I belonged," she says. "I remember once all these kids were lined up [in school] for vaccinations, and I was the only person who didn't have to because we were Christian Scientist. And even though I'm terrified of needles, I remember crying because I wanted to be in that line." [91]

Later, DeGeneres would use the feelings of being the new kid in school in her stand-up comedy routines, injecting them with her own brand of humor:

No, the kids were pretty nice. I mean, they would poke me with sticks and throw rocks and stuff, but I think that's normal. My parents did that, so who doesn't do it? Or they'd tease me: "Look who has a big head." But that's just normal—every dad does that. [92]

Real Hurt

In the spring of 1972, Elliott and Betty DeGeneres separated. They had not gotten along for some time, but had kept their troubles to themselves. It was a shock to both of their children, but it affected thirteen-year-old Ellen far more than her older brother. Vance was finished with high school and was living on his own. His day-to-day life would not change.

Betty moved out of the house to an apartment, taking Ellen with her. And while she was certain that splitting up the marriage was the right thing to do, she suffered some bouts of depression and self-doubt in the coming months. Interestingly, it was Ellen's humor that helped her get through those times. If Betty was surprised at her daughter's quick wit, Ellen today says she was even more so:

> The divorce helped me realize how important humor was. My mother was going through some really hard times. It's a hard adjustment to be a single mom and to go through everything she was. She was depressed—I don't even know why—but I could see when she was really getting down, so I would start to make fun of her dancing. Then she'd start to laugh and I'd make fun of her laughing. And she'd laugh so hard she'd start to cry, and then I'd make fun of that. . . . To be able, as a child, to make your mother who you look up to change her mood from depression to one of so much happiness is a very powerful thing . . . [and that] started pushing me towards comedy. [93]

To Texas

In 1973, after her divorce was final, Betty DeGeneres married again—this time to an electric company worker named Roy Gruessendorf. Ellen did not get along well with him; he was more strict than her mother had been, and was often critical of her and of the friends she had. In interviews she has been very closemouthed about Gruessendorf.

But during her sophomore year of high school, her mother was concerned that Ellen appeared to be drifting. She wasn't terribly interested

71

in school, preferring to daydream in classes that didn't interest her. She began hanging around with kids who were older, and she was becoming rebellious. For this reason, her mother agreed to move with her new husband to a little town in east Texas called Atlanta. Ellen would finish her sophomore year in New Orleans, living with her father; afterward, she would join her mother and stepfather in Texas.

Ellen made friends right away in her new surroundings. Coming from a large city like New Orleans made her something of a celebrity in little Atlanta. She knew that if all else failed, she could fall back on her sense of humor to make friends. "Instead of being the pretty girl who people flocked to," she said later, "I was the one who said something to make them pay attention." [94]

Because her family moved frequently, Ellen often felt anxious about fitting in at each new school.

Texas was something of a culture shock, however. The radio stations played country music instead of rock, and because there was so little for teens to do, drinking was very popular. So was something called "frog licking"—actually licking a frog to get high from a certain chemical found on its skin. Since these pastimes held no great appeal for Ellen, she got more involved in school activities than she had been in New Orleans. She sang in the school chorus and was voted Outstanding Player on her varsity tennis team.

A Serious Romance . . . and a Realization

Ellen, who had not dated much during her high school years, began to date Ben Heath, a handsome football star and top student at Atlanta High School. He enjoyed her sense of humor, and the two shared an interest in television comedies—especially NBC's new *Saturday Night Live.*

Their relationship grew more intense throughout their senior year, and that spring, they talked seriously about getting married. Ben gave her a promise ring, which had a small diamond in it; it was sort of a "engaged-to-be-engaged" symbol. But while Ellen had no immediate plans after graduating from Atlanta High School, Ben was planning on going to college. He thought it would be better not to rush into marriage.

Interestingly, Ben's suggestion that they wait forced DeGeneres to do some serious thinking of her own. Unlike many gay people, who sense early in life that they are attracted to people of the same sex, her own situation was different. She was only beginning to realize that she was far more attracted to women than men.

"I do like men," she says now. "People make choices all the time. Ben's now the mayor of some small town in Texas. I could be the mayor's wife. You know, I'm sure I'd have a nice place with Ben somewhere and we'd have kids and I wouldn't have known [that I was gay]. . . . But I would not be happy." [95]

No Direction

After high school, DeGeneres seemed to have no clear idea of what she wanted to do. She didn't think she wanted to go to college, since she didn't like studying very much. Being a veterinarian or a naturalist like Dian Fossey required far more education than she had. But the types of jobs available to someone without any college degree or specialized training were not jobs she wanted to do. She knew she couldn't make a living playing tennis. She had to admit to herself that she definitely lacked direction.

Ellen was voted Outstanding Player on her high school tennis team.

Although she and her mother were extremely close, DeGeneres felt that she needed to leave Texas. She decided to drive back to New Orleans and perhaps find something that appealed to her. De-Generes knew she could stay with her grandmother until she had money to get a place of her own.

She signed up for classes at the University of New Orleans, hoping to find a career. DeGeneres said later that she knew very quickly that college was not going to be any more interesting than high school had been. "I hated school," she remembered. "I started college

73

because everyone else was going. I majored in communications, I think. Or communications and drama. And I just remember sitting in there, and they were talking about the history of the Greek theater or something, and thinking, 'This is not what I want to know.'" [96]

Jobs and More Jobs

DeGeneres left school after half a semester and tried a number of different jobs. Some were so boring she lasted only a few hours; others she held for a few weeks or even several months. The point was to explore what jobs were out there and, of course, to make money.

She did clerical work in a law office, she worked in a car wash, and she baby-sat. She sold dresses at a store called the Merry-Go-Round, worked as an employment counselor, and sold vacuum cleaners. She was a restaurant hostess, a bartender, and an oyster shucker.

And while she didn't find anything she really enjoyed, DeGeneres did make a lot of new friends at each job. She was realizing that her sense of humor was entertaining to her friends, and she loved getting the laughs. She began writing humorous articles and features, and sent them to magazines like *National Lampoon* and *Ms*. Doing that felt more enjoyable than anything she'd done so far.

Telling the Secret

It was around this time in her life that DeGeneres decided to tell her parents that she was gay. She hadn't been sure for a long time, but she knew now that it was a part of who she was. She had had a few romantic relationships with women, and she sometimes visited the gay bars in New Orleans, where she felt she had met a supportive group of friends.

She told her mother first, when they were taking a walk along the beach. It was hard for her, because she knew her mother would be confused and possibly upset by the revelation. After all, her mother had grown up in a time when it was assumed that girls grew up and got married.

But if Betty DeGeneres was disapproving or unhappy, she didn't show it to Ellen. She was surprised and a little concerned about her daughter's future. But she knew there was nothing she could do to change things. Said DeGeneres later, "The most ironic thing about this was that her whole fear was, 'You're not going to meet a man? Who's going to take care of you?'" [97]

Unfortunately, telling her father was not as easy. He was remarried, with two young stepdaughters, and Ellen told him during a visit when she was staying at his house. When she told her father, he and his wife told her she should leave. He wasn't angry with DeGeneres, but he

DeGeneres began her comedy career in 1980, performing at a university coffeehouse.

and his wife thought the little girls would be in jeopardy with her there. Such an assumption was hurtful to DeGeneres; however, she realized his decision was based on ignorance of what homosexuality is, rather than on meanness. But she decided to keep the secret from the rest of the family, at least for the time being.

On Stage

In 1980, DeGeneres finally realized what she wanted to do with her life—and this revelation came about quite by accident. Some people she knew were putting together a benefit in the French Quarter of New Orleans and needed entertainment. So many of her friends thought she could be a comic if she'd just give it a try, but until then, she had just shrugged off their suggestions. However, here was a chance to get onstage and be funny.

She agreed, and to her surprise, she not only enjoyed herself but also got a good response from the audience. One person invited her to do comedy at a coffeehouse on the campus of the University of New Orleans, and she accepted. Luckily, she had files of the little articles she'd been writing and submitting to magazines, so she had plenty of material. These little items weren't really jokes, like other comics told. They were more like ramblings, with strategic pauses and funny expressions she made as she talked:

> I ask people why they have deer heads on their walls, and they say, "Because it's such a beautiful animal." There you go. Well, I think my mother's attractive, but I have *photographs* of her. . . . I tell you, the deer heads that I feel sorry for the most are the ones on the walls of bars or restaurants. They have the silly party hats on them, silly sunglasses, streamers around their necks. These are the ones I feel sorry for. I mean, obviously, they were at a party having a good time. They were in there dancing to their little deer music, "A crossbow will make ya JUMP—JUMP!" Then, all of a sudden . . . *ker-plow!* . . . the party's over. [98]

After her job at the university coffeehouse, she began to get other offers. She appeared at other coffeehouses and small clubs in the New Orleans area. The pay was minimal—often less than twenty dollars for the evening. But it was money she was tremendously proud of. At last, she was doing what she really enjoyed.

A Sad Setback

During this time, DeGeneres had been living with a woman named Kat. She was someone about whom DeGeneres felt deeply, someone she wanted to be with for a very long time. Unfortunately, Kat was killed in a car accident on the interstate highway near their apartment. Like most young people, DeGeneres had not yet had experiences with such loss, and it devastated her.

But as she had done in other times of crisis, she found a way to use her strength—her humor. She wrote what came to be one of her most popular bits, a funny-sad telephone conversation between herself and God. It was her way of questioning things that were far beyond her control, and while it was not rolling-in-the-aisles funny, it struck a responsive chord with her audiences.

As she tried to get her emotions back on track, DeGeneres auditioned for a new comedy club opening in New Orleans called Clyde's Comedy Corner. The owner hoped to make Clyde's nationally known, the sort of place where hot new comics would gain recognition. He hired Ellen on the spot, and beginning in December 1980, she was appearing at the club for one show every night during the week and two shows on Friday and Saturday nights. She would have lots of opportunities to polish her act, seeing what worked and what didn't. And best of all, she would be making enough money at it so that she didn't have to work to support her "comedy hobby."

Fame

As she continued to have success at Clyde's, other comics who came to town were astonished that she had not yet taken her act on the road. She finally got the message when a friend moved to San Francisco and told Ellen about all the comedy clubs and how beautiful the city was. Convinced that she would conquer the West Coast as she had conquered New Orleans, DeGeneres moved to San Francisco.

However, there were dozens of comedy clubs and hundreds of comics looking for work. She quickly realized that while the city was indeed beautiful, it was not ready to welcome a newcomer, no matter how well known she'd been in New Orleans. Feeling defeated, she moved back to New Orleans. Clyde's Comedy Corner had closed because of poor financial management, and she was back doing odd jobs.

Cable television turned things around for DeGeneres. Cable TV in the 1980s had become the most popular medium for showcasing new comics, and she was at an advantage. She had already polished her act and was very self-confident. In fact, she was voted Funniest Person in America on a Showtime cable competition. From then on, she was considered a hot commodity—and it seemed that American audiences couldn't get enough of Ellen DeGeneres.

An Honest Comedian

Her fans enjoyed her comedy because they felt as though she was not trying to make them laugh. She seemed to be merely talking honestly about things that interested, annoyed, or puzzled her. One popular routine had to do with elevator etiquette:

> We always do this: we walk up to an elevator, someone's already there, they're waiting, they've pushed the button, the button is lit. We walk up and push the button, thinking, "Obviously you didn't push it correctly. I'll have to push it myself. *Now* the elevator will come." Then someone else walks up and they push the button again. Suddenly, you're offended. You want to say, "You idiot, I pushed it, he pushed it." Then, to the original pusher, "Can you believe people?"

Or, if you go to the elevator by yourself, you push the button, you wait for the elevator to come, the elevator doesn't come. You push the button six more times. Like that's helping. As if the elevator's thinking, "Oh, a half dozen people are there now. I better hurry. I thought it was just that one woman. I was resting. Oh no, I . . . , I could lose my job! I could become stairs!"[99]

A Show of Her Own

Following very successful appearances on such popular programs as *The Tonight Show* and *David Letterman,* DeGeneres was given small parts in a few short-lived sitcoms. And while the sitcoms themselves did not do well, she was gaining experience and camera time.

In 1993, she signed a deal to do a pilot for a season-replacement program to be called *These Friends of Mine.* Its premise was a single woman living with several friends and the situations that develop. Because it was built around DeGeneres, it was taken seriously because of the success of another comedian in a "show about nothing"—Jerry Seinfeld. The creators of the show believed that Ellen's wit and likable nature would make strict plot lines unnecessary.

DeGeneres was excited about the show and tried to make the main character a more exaggerated version of herself. "I think the character . . . is a lot more naive and a little more gullible than I am," she explained. "I put my foot in my mouth sometimes and realize, 'Oh, man, that was the wrong thing to say' and try to backpedal out of it. But the character I play is *constantly* doing that. She's self-conscious, but at the same time she'll do anything. She's a goon, but yet, there's an intelligence behind this gooniness."[100]

Ending Speculation

The show received generally positive feedback from audiences and critics alike. It went through some changes; its title became *Ellen,* and gradually the episodes began to fit her comedy style extremely well. There were cast changes, too, as well as a shuffling of the show's day and time. But it had a loyal following, and its ratings remained strong.

In 1996, DeGeneres was feeling unsettled about the series and perhaps about herself. Rumors had been circulating about her sexual identity, and while in the past she had been able to smile and deflect such rumors with a wisecrack or a "I don't discuss my private life" comment, she didn't want to do those things anymore. She decided to reveal that she was gay—to come out—and in the process, have her character in the show do the same.

Hints about the event leaked to the press, and "Is she or isn't she?" was a large topic of debate in the months before the show. By the time the much talked about episode was aired on April 30, 1997, De-Generes had acknowledged that she was gay and that her character would be acknowledging the same thing.

"I Never Felt Like I Belonged Anywhere"

Although coming out was a highly controversial move for television, she said that she was glad she no longer had to pretend to be someone she wasn't. For years, she explained, she felt isolated, even among fellow comedians. "You can imagine the fag jokes," she said in a 1997 interview. "When I started headlining, it was always guys on before me. I would always follow somebody doing either dyke jokes or fag jokes and doing the lisp thing. . . . I just thought, 'Oh, God, what if they pick up that I'm gay?' It was that fear and shame. I never felt like I belonged anywhere." [101]

The cast of Ellen, *which was the first television series to feature a gay character in a lead role, poses for a publicity shot.*

Gay-rights supporters gather to watch the Ellen *episode in which DeGeneres's character comes out as a lesbian.*

Reaction to the show was mixed, which was expected. Two of the show's sponsors decided to pull their advertising, for they did not wish to lose customers over such a controversial issue. And although many viewers had difficulty with DeGeneres being gay, she says that she received a great amount of support from both fans and her show business peers.

Most of all, she was eager for the media frenzy to die down. Not only were people interested in the character she played, they were becoming very interested in DeGeneres's own love life, especially when she began a relationship with actress Anne Heche.

DeGeneres insisted that while she knew that coming out was right for her, she didn't intend for her sexual orientation to define her. "I mean, I understand the curiosity and I understand the not understanding of it," she explained. "Because I didn't understand for a long time, and I'm still struggling to—I have the same problems that a lot of people do. But let's get beyond this, and let me get back to what I do."[102]

Ellen DeGeneres is certainly not the only lesbian comedian in show business. In fact, there are many who make their sexual orientation a large part of their act. DeGeneres is not one of these; though she has come out by way of her television character, she is determined not to become stereotyped by such a private aspect of her life. The television episode that gave audiences an opportunity to understand how difficult coming out can be was a brave undertaking for a woman who continues to be defined by the humor she finds in all aspects of life.

NOTES

Introduction: The Rule Breakers

1. Susan Horowitz, *Queens of Comedy: Lucille Ball, Phyllis Diller, Carol Burnett, Joan Rivers, and the New Generation of Funny Women*. Amsterdam: Gordon and Breach, 1997, p. i.

2. Quoted in Nancy A. Walker, *A Very Serious Thing: Women's Humor and American Culture*. Minneapolis: University of Minnesota Press, 1988, p. 74.

3. Quoted in Linda Martin and Kerry Segrave, *Women in Comedy: The Funny Ladies from the Turn of the Century to the Present*. Secaucus, NJ: Citadel Press, 1986, p. 14.

4. Quoted in Martin and Segrave, *Women in Comedy*, p. 13.

5. Quoted in Martin and Segrave, *Women in Comedy*, p. 14.

6. Martin and Segrave, *Women in Comedy*, p. 18.

7. Quoted in Horowitz, *Queens of Comedy*, p. 5.

8. Bob Epstein, personal interview with the author, July 22, 2001, Minneapolis, MN.

Chapter 1: Gracie Allen

9. Quoted in George Burns, *Gracie: A Love Story*. New York: Putnam, 1998, p. 25.

10. Quoted in J. K. Morris, "Gracie Allen's Own Story: Inside Me," *Woman's Home Companion*, March 1953, p. 100.

11. Quoted in Morris, "Gracie Allen's Own Story," p. 41.

12. Quoted in Morris, "Gracie Allen's Own Story," p. 102.

13. Quoted in Morris, "Gracie Allen's Own Story," p. 109.

14. Quoted in Shirley Staples, *Male-Female Comedy Teams in American Vaudeville, 1865–1932*. Ann Arbor, MI: UMI Research Press, 1984, p. 222.

15. Quoted in Morris, "Gracie Allen's Own Story," p. 116.

16. Quoted in Staples, *Male-Female Comedy Teams*, p. 214.

17. Quoted in Morris, "Gracie Allen's Own Story," p. 121.

18. Quoted in Martin and Segrave, *Women in Comedy*, p. 145.

19. Quoted in Cheryl Blythe and Susan Sackett, *Say Goodnight, Gracie! The Story of Burns and Allen*. New York: Dutton, 1986, pp. 18–19.

20. Quoted in Morris, "Gracie Allen's Own Story," p. 123.

21. Quoted in Burns, *Gracie,* p. 161.

Chapter 2: Lucille Ball

22. Quoted in Kathleen Brady, *Lucille: The Life of Lucille Ball.* New York: Billboard Books, 2001, p. 7.

23. Quoted in Michael McClay, *I Love Lucy: The Complete Picture History of the Most Popular TV Show Ever.* New York: Time-Warner, 1995, p. 4.

24. Quoted in Martin and Segrave, *Women in Comedy,* p. 263.

25. Quoted in Martin and Segrave, *Women in Comedy,* p. 263.

26. Quoted in Karin Adir, *The Great Clowns of American Television.* Jefferson, NC: McFarland, 1988, p. 2.

27. Quoted in Horowitz, *Queens of Comedy,* p. 22.

28. Quoted in Horowitz, *Queens of Comedy,* p. 22.

29. Quoted in McClay, *I Love Lucy,* p. 10.

30. Quoted in Stephen Silverman, *Funny Ladies.* New York: Abrams, 1999, p. 74.

31. Quoted in Jim Brochu, *Lucy in the Afternoon: An Intimate Memoir of Lucille Ball.* New York: Morrow, 1990, p. 102.

32. Quoted in Martin and Segrave, *Women in Comedy,* p. 270.

33. Quoted in Martin and Segrave, *Women in Comedy,* p. 273.

34. Quoted in Brochu, *Lucy in the Afternoon,* p. 143.

35. Quoted in Adir, *The Great Clowns of American Television,* p. 20.

36. Quoted in Coyne Steven Sanders and Tom Gilbert, *Desilu: The Story of Lucille Ball and Desi Arnaz.* New York: Morrow, 1993, p. 212.

37. Quoted in Sanders and Gilbert, *Desilu,* p. 216.

38. Quoted in Martin and Segrave, *Women in Comedy,* p. 275.

39. Quoted in Brady, *Lucille,* p. 332.

40. Quoted in McClay, *I Love Lucy,* p. 114.

Chapter 3: Whoopi Goldberg

41. Quoted in *People Weekly,* "Whoopi Goldberg: Stand-Up Comedienne," May 28, 1984, p. 72.

42. Whoopi Goldberg, *Book.* New York: Weisbach Books, 1997, p. 3.

43. Quoted in James Robert Parish, *Whoopi Goldberg: Her Journey from Poverty to Mega-Stardom.* Secaucus, NJ: Birch Lane Press, 1997, p. 21.

44. Quoted in Parish, *Whoopi Goldberg*, p. 24.

45. Parish, *Whoopi Goldberg*, p. 24.

46. Goldberg, *Book*, p. 39.

47. Goldberg, *Book*, p. 40.

48. Quoted in Parish, *Whoopi Goldberg*, p. 31.

49. Goldberg, *Book*, pp. 40–41.

50. Quoted in Parish, *Whoopi Goldberg*, p. 27.

51. Quoted in Parish, *Whoopi Goldberg*, p. 28.

52. Quoted in Parish, *Whoopi Goldberg*, p. 27.

53. Quoted in Parish, *Whoopi Goldberg*, pp. 29–30.

54. Quoted in Parish, *Whoopi Goldberg*, p. 36.

55. Quoted in Parish, *Whoopi Goldberg*, p. 36.

56. Quoted in Parish, *Whoopi Goldberg*, p. 39.

57. Quoted in Parish, *Whoopi Goldberg*, p. 43.

58. Quoted in Laura B. Randolph, "The Whoopi Goldberg Nobody Knows," *Ebony*, March 1991, p. 110.

59. Quoted in Parish, *Whoopi Goldberg*, p. 97.

60. Quoted in Parish, *Whoopi Goldberg*, p. 116.

61. Quoted in Parish, *Whoopi Goldberg*, p. 116.

62. Quoted in Parish, *Whoopi Goldberg*, p. 119.

63. Quoted in Parish, *Whoopi Goldberg*, p. 124.

64. Quoted in Kim Cunningham, "Grandma Misbehaves," *People Weekly*, November 11, 1996, p. 174.

65. Quoted in Parish, *Whoopi Goldberg*, p. 221.

66. Quoted in Parish, *Whoopi Goldberg*, p. 217.

67. Quoted in Parish, *Whoopi Goldberg*, p. 337.

68. Quoted in Lisa Russell, "Peeling Off the Label," *People Weekly*, August 22, 1994, p. 126.

Chapter 4: Roseanne

69. Quoted in Geraldine Barr, *My Sister Roseanne: The True Story of Roseanne Barr Arnold*. Secaucus, NJ: Birch Lane Press, 1994, p. 135.

70. Lawrence Christon, "Roseanne Live: Icon of the Spit-Curl Set," *Los Angeles Times*, February 24, 1990.

71. Quoted in Elaine Dutka, "Roseanne Barr: Slightly to the Left of Normal," *Time*, May 8, 1989, p. 82.

72. Quoted in Gioia Diliberto, "Lampooning Domestic War, Comedienne Roseanne Barr Has Gone Far by Being Bizarre," *People Weekly,* April 28, 1986, p. 105.

73. Barr, *My Sister Roseanne,* p. 40.

74. Barr, *My Sister Roseanne,* p. 26.

75. Roseanne Barr, *My Life as a Woman.* New York: Harper and Row, 1989, p. 44.

76. Barr, *My Life as a Woman,* p. 10.

77. Barr, *My Life as a Woman,* p. 38.

78. Barr, *My Life as a Woman,* pp. 84–85.

79. Barr, *My Sister Roseanne,* p. 62.

80. Barr, *My Life as a Woman,* p. 144.

81. Barr, *My Life as a Woman,* p. 165.

82. Barr, *My Life as a Woman,* p. 166.

83. Quoted in Barr, *My Sister Roseanne,* pp. 135–36.

84. Barr, *My Life as a Woman,* p. 3.

85. Barr, *My Life as a Woman,* p. 5.

86. Quoted in Richard Zoglin, "Roseanne," *Time,* December 5, 1988, p. 88.

87. Quoted in Christine Gorman and Barbara Dolan, "Incest Comes Out of the Dark," *Time,* October 7, 1991, p. 46.

Chapter 5: Ellen DeGeneres

88. Quoted in Bruce Handy, "He Called Me Degenerate?" *Time,* April 14, 1997, p. 86.

89. Quoted in Kathleen Tracy, *Ellen: The Real Story of Ellen DeGeneres.* Secaucus, NJ: Birch Lane Press, 1999, p. 6.

90. Quoted in Tracy, *Ellen,* p. 8.

91. Quoted in Tracy, *Ellen,* p. 9.

92. Quoted in Tracy, *Ellen,* p. 10.

93. Quoted in Tracy, *Ellen,* pp. 11–12.

94. Quoted in R. Daniel Foster, "Newgirl," *Los Angeles Magazine,* October 1994, p. 32.

95. Quoted in Tracy, *Ellen,* p. 20.

96. Quoted in Liz Scott, "Ellen DeGeneres," *New Orleans Magazine,* July 1994, p. 68.

97. Quoted in Tracy, *Ellen,* p. 31.

98. Ellen DeGeneres, *My Point . . . And I Do Have One.* New York: Bantam Books, 1995, p. 147.

99. DeGeneres, *My Point,* pp. 190–91.

100. Quoted in Tracy, *Ellen,* p. 84.

101. Quoted in Handy, "He Called Me Degenerate?" p. 86.

102. Quoted in Handy, "He Called Me Degenerate?" p. 87.

FOR FURTHER READING

Lucille Ball, *Love, Lucy.* New York: Putnam, 1996. Excellent information on her youth.

George Burns and Cynthia Hobart Lindsay, *I Love Her, That's Why! An Autobiography.* New York: Simon and Schuster, 1955. Good anecdotes, well organized.

Judy De Boer, *Whoopi Goldberg.* Mankato, MN: Creative Education, 1999. Superb color photographs; less detail than other books about her, but terse and interesting.

Ann G. Gaines, *Roseanne.* Philadelphia: Chelsea House, 1998. Good chronology and index.

———, *Whoopi Goldberg.* Philadelphia: Chelsea House, 1999. Good photographs from many of her movies. Detailed list of all her film, television, and theater work.

Mary Unterbrink, *Funny Women: American Comediennes, 1860–1985.* Jefferson, NC: McFarland, 1987. Helpful information on role of women in show business, starting in vaudeville days.

Works Consulted

Books

Karin Adir, *The Great Clowns of American Television*. Jefferson, NC: McFarland, 1988. Well written, with a helpful index.

Roseanne Arnold, *My Lives*. New York: Ballantine Books, 1994. Adult language, some helpful background information on her television show.

Geraldine Barr, *My Sister Roseanne: The True Story of Roseanne Barr Arnold*. Secaucus, NJ: Birch Lane Press, 1994. Very good information about Roseanne's family background; helpful index.

Roseanne Barr, *My Life as a Woman*. New York: Harper and Row, 1989. Adult language, but helpful background information on Roseanne's life before she became famous.

Cheryl Blythe and Susan Sackett, *Say Goodnight, Gracie! The Story of Burns and Allen*. New York: Dutton, 1986. Lots of detail about the television years of Burns and Allen; helpful index.

Kathleen Brady, *Lucille: The Life of Lucille Ball*. New York: Billboard Books, 2001. Difficult reading for younger readers, but some excellent pictures and behind-the-scenes anecdotes from *I Love Lucy*.

Jim Brochu, *Lucy in the Afternoon: An Intimate Memoir of Lucille Ball*. New York: Morrow, 1990. Highly interesting information about Ball's later life; excellent photos not seen in other books.

George Burns, *Gracie: A Love Story*. New York: Putnam, 1998. Good insight into Burns's years in show business with Gracie Allen; good anecdotes not found in other sources.

Betty DeGeneres, *Love, Ellen: A Mother/Daughter Journey*. New York: Weisbach Books, 1999. Excellent glimpses into daughter Ellen's childhood and teenage years.

Ellen DeGeneres, *My Point . . . And I Do Have One*. New York: Bantam Books, 1995. Snippets of comedy routines mixed in with autobiographical information.

Whoopi Goldberg, *Book*. New York: Weisbach Books, 1997. Many adult topics, but good information about her early life in New York City.

Susan Horowitz, *Queens of Comedy: Lucille Ball, Phyllis Diller, Carol Burnett, Joan Rivers, and the New Generation of Funny Women*. Amsterdam: Gordon and Breach, 1997. Well researched, with helpful bibliography.

Linda Martin and Kerry Segrave, *Women in Comedy: The Funny Ladies from the Turn of the Century to the Present.* Secaucus, NJ: Citadel Press, 1986. Excellent introduction on problems women have had doing comedy. Good chapter on Gracie Allen.

Michael McClay, *I Love Lucy: The Complete Picture History of the Most Popular TV Show Ever.* New York: Time-Warner, 1995. Interesting foreword by Ball's daughter; excellent insights into her personal life.

James Robert Parish, *Whoopi Goldberg: Her Journey from Poverty to Mega-Stardom.* Secaucus, NJ: Birch Lane Press, 1997. Excellent quotations and helpful bibliography.

Coyne Steven Sanders and Tom Gilbert, *Desilu: The Story of Lucille Ball and Desi Arnaz.* New York: Morrow, 1993. More adult in content, but good background on her marriage to Arnaz.

Stephen Silverman, *Funny Ladies.* New York: Abrams, 1999. Basic information; well-organized segment on Lucille Ball.

Shirley Staples, *Male-Female Comedy Teams in American Vaudeville, 1865–1932.* Ann Arbor, MI: UMI Research Press, 1984. A basic look at the Burns and Allen comedy team, but with sparse detail.

Kathleen Tracy, *Ellen: The Real Story of Ellen DeGeneres.* Secaucus, NJ: Birch Lane Press, 1999. Excellent information and helpful index.

Nancy A. Walker, *A Very Serious Thing: Women's Humor and American Culture.* Minneapolis: University of Minnesota Press, 1988. Excellent background; complete bibliography.

Periodicals

Lawrence Christon, "Roseanne Live: Icon of the Spit-Curl Set," *Los Angeles Times,* February 24, 1990.

Kim Cunningham, "Grandma Misbehaves," *People Weekly,* November 11, 1996.

Hilary De Vries, "Funny Girl: Ellen Is DeGeneres to a Fault—and That's Why We Like Her," *Ladies Home Journal,* May 1995.

Gioia Diliberto, "Lampooning Domestic War, Comedienne Roseanne Barr Has Gone Far by Being Bizarre," *People Weekly,* April 28, 1986.

Elaine Dutka, "Roseanne Barr: Slightly to the Left of Normal," *Time,* May 8, 1989.

R. Daniel Foster, "Newgirl," *Los Angeles Magazine,* October 1994.

Christine Gorman and Barbara Dolan, "Incest Comes Out of the Dark," *Time,* October 7, 1991.

Bruce Handy, "He Called Me Degenerate?" *Time,* April 14, 1997.

J. K. Morris, "Gracie Allen's Own Story: Inside Me," *Woman's Home Companion*, March 1953.

People Weekly, "Whoopi Goldberg: Stand-Up Comedienne," May 28, 1984.

Laura B. Randolph, "The Whoopi Goldberg Nobody Knows," *Ebony*, March 1991.

Lisa Russell, "Peeling Off the Label," *People Weekly*, August 22, 1994.

Liz Scott, "Ellen DeGeneres," *New Orleans Magazine*, July 1994.

Richard Zoglin, "Roseanne," *Time*, December 5, 1988.

PICTURE CREDITS

ABOUT THE AUTHOR

Gail B. Stewart received her undergraduate degree from Gustavus Adolphus College in St. Peter, Minnesota. She did her graduate work in English, linguistics, and curriculum study at the college of St. Thomas and the University of Minnesota. She taught English and reading for more than ten years.

She has written over ninety books for young people, including a series for Lucent Books called the Other America. She has written many books on historical topics such as World War I and the Warsaw ghetto.

Stewart and her husband live in Minneapolis with their three sons, Ted, Elliot, and Flynn; two dogs; and a cat. When she is not writing, she enjoys reading, walking, and watching her sons play soccer.